Til Death Do Us Part

Award Winning Author

JAN SIKES

RiJan
PUBLISHING

RiJan Publishing

Cover Design by Donna Osborn Clark at: creationbydonna.com

Interior Design and Typesetting by: interiorbookdesigns.com

ISBN 978-0-9906179-4-5

Published by:

RIJAN PUBLISHING

www.rijanpublishing.com

This book, the final segment of the series, is dedicated to the life and times of James R. (Rick) Sikes, 8-5-35 – 5-1-09. If not for him, and his story, there would be no books. I know he is proud of my accomplishments. As he so often said, he is still around even though his body isn't and I know he has shared in the triumphs with me from Spirit world.

Someone who has stood beside me since the beginning of this journey is my best friend in life, Kay Shields Perot. You may know her as Sally in the books. She has always encouraged me, cheered me on and picked me up when I faltered. Thank you from the bottom of my heart, Kay!

Jan Sikes

~Luke Stone and his beloved Martin D-35 guitar~

Reviewer Quotes

I recommend the entire series for readers who want to experience a true love story that shows how caring for each other, commitment and working together results in lives well lived. Jan's passion for detail and raw style make this autobiography a must read!

~ C. Schartz, Missouri

The characters depicted are real people, and this is their story. It's both tragic and triumphant. It exhibits the depth the human spirit can reach in order to not only survive, but also thrive. And it exemplifies the long-held truth that believing makes it so. Energy follows thought. And Luke and Darlina show us how to manifest our heart's desire.

~ T. Frisco, California

Jan Sikes' powerful "autobiographical fiction" novels, featuring Darlina and Luke, are a moving mixture of erotic love, successes and heartbreak.

~ S. Stuart, UK

I loved this book and well as the two before it. This story shows how love can survive anything if you are willing to try.

~ A. Melvin, Louisiana

Darlina and Luke went through a lot of difficulties and struggles but persevered. A love like theirs is very rare. I highly recommend this book

~ E. Rainbird, Australia

Although some creative liberties have been taken, this novel is based on real people — Rick and Jan Sikes — and real events.

~FOREWORD~

Linda Broday

USA Today and NY Times Bestselling Author

Stricken with rheumatic fever, Luke Stone remained bedfast for two years as a young boy. It took a toll on his spirit, but perhaps this helped to prepare him for a life full of ups and downs. He survived this disease and grew into a strong young man.

At the age of fourteen, his uncle gave him a guitar. This ignited a passion that lasted a lifetime.

His first time on stage at the age of fifteen left a memory time could not erase. The quaking of his knees knocking together almost drowned out the music. He lay awake in his bed that night thinking about the experience until the wee hours of morning. The next weekend, he went back for more. He continued on, eventually putting together a band that gained a great level of popularity across the state of Texas and beyond.

In his twenties and on into his thirties, he built several reputations. He and his brother, Bobby, became known as the toughest men around West Central Texas. Luke claimed the title as King of the Texas Honkytonks and was recognized far and wide as a notorious lady's man.

But, a bad decision put him behind bars in Leavenworth Prison for fifteen years. This took a lot out of him. No longer was he the bull-in-the-china-closet that kicked ass and took names.

With music as his solace, through the long years of incarceration, he wrote hundreds of songs and even managed to advocate for a recording studio inside the prison. He had a burning desire to get some of these songs to the outside world.

When the long awaited parole came and he headed home, he hung up his neon dreams for a hammer and paint brush. He had a new family to take care of and vowed that it wouldn't include playing music in the Texas honkytonks. He put his guitar in the closet and went about the business of building a home and helping raise the two girls his beloved Darlina brought with her into the marriage. How he loved having a second chance at being a daddy and teaching them to be strong responsible young ladies!

In this part of the story, he's now been out of prison as long as he'd been in…fifteen years.

As detailed in previous books, there were hard times aplenty and many struggles that brought both Luke and Darlina to their knees more than once, but, they faced them together. True partners both in body and soul, their steadfast love carried them through the best and the worst life threw their way.

Even with the health issues that plagued Luke, he often thought there had never been a man born as lucky as him. Sometimes, it felt as though he'd lived several lifetimes all rolled into this one.

And he wasn't done yet. He never tried to fool himself or anyone else. He knew the sand running through his hourglass was growing thin, but that didn't matter either. He vowed to make the very best of every day, every minute he had left. And who was to say that he wouldn't live to be an old, old man with lots of stories to tell?

None of that mattered. Only the day given to him was the most important thing.

For each moment that remained, he had another chance to build something, write something, or imagine something that he hadn't yet done. Determined to leave a rich, lasting legacy, the prints of his shoes are still being seen.

And that is the true beauty of living.

Chapter 1

Luke Stone pulled his Martin D-35 guitar out of its case and settled onto a chair. His gaze took in the walls of the redneck double-wide trailer house he'd put together from bits and pieces of nothing over the past fifteen years.

Funny, but it seemed he'd been doing that all of his life, taking scraps and turning them into treasures. He couldn't help being proud of his accomplishments.

He'd worn many different hats in his sixty-five years of living. But one had never changed for as long as he could remember. He had been born to write songs and play music.

With the guitar tuned, he strummed a chord and relished the ring of the strings.

The year 2000, the year doomsayers predicted the world to end. Luke couldn't buy that, although he never dreamed he'd live to see a new millennium.

It had ended for his friend and spirit brother, Roxy Gordon, a couple of months back when he died from cirrhosis of the liver. And yet through that ending came another beginning for Luke. Another chance to pull his guitar out of the closet and revive the deep passion he had for music.

He turned his attention to the words of the songs that played through his fingers. Halfway through the third ballad, he looked up as Darlina, the queen of his heart with sparkling blue eyes that saw only the best in him, waltzed through the door. The bright sunlight reflected off her auburn hair seconds before the door closed and his breath caught somewhere deep in his chest. How was it possible that she could still do that to him after fifteen years of marriage?

He stuck the guitar pick between the top two strings and rested his beloved Martin on a stand. He wanted nothing more than to fill his arms with her warm tender spirit.

By the time she tossed her purse and keys onto the table, Luke stood beside her.

"Hi, baby," He inhaled the flowered scent of her hair.

"Hi, yourself." She turned her face upward to receive his kiss. "You didn't have to stop playing just because I came home. You know how I love to listen and how happy I am that you finally brought your guitar out of hiding."

"For the life of me I can't figure why, but for you I'll keep playing." Luke let his hands slide to her rounded bottom before letting go and walking from the den into the kitchen, arm-in-arm.

Back in his chair, he reached for the Martin, his eyes never leaving Darlina, as she opened the refrigerator and turned on the stove. He thought of how she'd believed in him when he could find no reasons left to believe in himself. For the millionth time, he wished they'd met sooner. Maybe then he could have avoided wasting fifteen long years in Leavenworth prison.

She'd been a breath of fresh air when their paths crossed in Abilene, Texas in 1970. Barely nineteen, naïve and trusting, she was entirely different from the women who hung around the bars and honkytonks where he played. But, it was too little, too late. The die had been cast.

He shook his head as if to clear the memories. That was then and this is now. Thirty years had changed him from the arrogant, rebellious King of the Honkytonks to a man with purpose. He'd happily hung up his neon dreams to be a worthy husband to Darlina and father to two little blond-haired blue-eyed girls who were now successful and strong young women. Being given a new lease on life, on the music he loved and on the woman he adored far exceeded his wildest dreams. He damned well intended to take full advantage of it every day for the rest of his time on earth.

"Play something you wrote." Darlina's voice brought him back from the reverie. He looked up to see a wide smile.

He chuckled. "Okay. Here's a new one I'm workin' on. It's not finished yet."

"Perfect." She turned back to the stove.

He thumbed through a tablet and landed on a fresh page. He cleared his throat, sipped from his tea glass then strummed.

"I think it's over and then memories set in
Ah, but it's dying bit by bit
While I cling desperately to it.
Slowly, the last love dies

Lingering after echoes of final goodbyes
Slowly, oh slowly last love dies.
Sometimes love seems forever
Sometimes it is pleasure
Sometimes love is slow
Sometimes it's fast
But one thing for certain I know
Someday some love will be the last."

He continued to play and hum, stopping to write on the tablet now and again.

Finally, he stopped. "Well, what do you think?"

Darlina joined him and draped her arm across his shoulders. "I think it's good, but sad, sweetheart."

Luke sighed. "Not everyone has happiness in life. Lord knows I've only found it in the last fifteen years." He laid his callused hand on her soft one.

She leaned down and kissed the top of his head.

He carefully placed the guitar back on its stand and pulled her onto his lap. "I mean it, honey. I've had a lifetime of hardships and sadness. I've been a tough guy, played on big stages all across the country, had lots of women and drank lots of whiskey. But, nothing is better than what I have right now in this ragged ol' pieced-together trailer house with you."

Darlina rested her head on his shoulder. "I'll never forget how scared I was when Dr. Robertson told me you'd had a heart attack and needed open heart surgery. Somehow I just couldn't let myself believe that we'd waited so long to build a life together only to have it ripped away after three short years."

"And now look at us, almost twelve years later and I'm still here. As long as I have a breath in my body, I'll keep building and working for us." Luke stroked her hair.

Darlina sighed. "I've always been a believer in miracles and now for you to be writing and playing music again. Well, it's just another of those miracles I hoped for and believed in."

"Yep, you and me both." Luke twitched his nose. "What's that smell?"

"Oh shit! I forgot I was cooking." She jumped off his lap and made a beeline for the kitchen.

Luke laughed out loud.

"It's not funny. You may be eating a sandwich for supper."

"Hell, I don't care as long as I'm eating it with you."

Darlina grabbed the pan from the stove and plunked it into the sink. "It's your fault, you know. You made me forget what I was doing."

"And I intend to do that every chance I get." Luke chuckled.

Just then a knock came on the side door and before either Luke or Darlina could open it, Judy Gordon entered with a tall, slender man close behind her.

"I hope I'm not interrupting y'all." Judy said, laying her purse on the table.

Darlina hugged her. "Of course not. Come on in."

Luke stood and embraced Judy. "What are you up to, sugar?"

"Luke, Darlina, this is a friend of mine and Roxy's, Frank Cambert."

Luke shook his hand. "Nice to meet you, Frank. Can I offer you guys something to drink?"

"Got a cold beer?" Judy asked.

"Of course. Frank, can I bring you a beer too?" Darlina wiped her hands on a kitchen towel.

Frank smiled and nodded.

"Have a seat." Luke moved to his recliner.

Judy sat on the sofa and Frank chose a chair across from Luke.

"Judy's told me a lot about you, Luke. I've known Roxy and Judy since the days they lived in California. I just got word of Roxy's death and made a trip to see Judy. I still can't believe he's gone."

Luke shook his head. "I know, man. I can't either. I think about him every day."

Judy accepted the beer Darlina handed her and popped the tab to open it. "You and me both, Luke. I don't know how I'm going to live without Roxy." Tears filled her eyes.

Luke leaned forward, placing a comforting hand on her shoulder. "We'll help you, Judy."

She sniffed. "Luke, would you play some music for Frank? He wants to hear some songs you wrote and maybe you can tell him a story or two from your days on the road."

"Aw, Judy. I don't want to bore him."

"Truly, it wouldn't be boring, Luke. I sincerely want to hear some of your music and I know you've got tales to tell."

"I hate to interrupt, but I was making our supper and burned it, so I'm going to put together some sandwiches. Have you guys eaten?" Darlina asked.

"No, but we don't want to be any trouble. Y'all go ahead. I just want to drink a beer." Judy's hand trembled as she brought the can up to her lips.

"It's no bother. We've got plenty." Darlina turned back to the kitchen while Luke reached for his guitar.

"Any requests?" He slung the guitar strap across his shoulders.

"I have one," Judy said. "Play *Den of Sin*."

Luke strummed.

"I'm going down to where they call me Goodtime Charlie
To drink all my troubles away
To the place where my good times all started
But they're over because she's coming home today
Den of sin, den of sin, for us this is the end
No more staying out and laying up all day.
I'm not crying because my baby left me.
I'm crying 'cause she's coming home to stay."

Once the song came to an end, both Frank and Judy applauded.

"That's a tear-jerker in reverse," Luke drawled. "He ain't cryin' 'cause she's leavin'. He's cryin' 'cause she's comin' back."

Frank chuckled. "Nice twist."

"It's the only number one song I ever had. It made it all the way to the top of the charts in Denmark back in the 60s." Luke chuckled. "I figure Denmark's about the size of Coleman County, but, they liked my song."

"How many years did you work the road?" Frank asked.

"Oh lord. I got on stage for the first time when I was fifteen. I was a big ol' dumb farm kid, but I had a by-god guitar and I wanted to sing. It was out here at the Coleman City Park. There were some older guys that my mom and dad knew and they asked me to get up and sing. Hell, my knees were knocking together so hard, I could hardly hear myself. Somehow I got through it and didn't stop until I got carted away to Federal Finishing School twenty some-odd years later."

"Judy told me about you going to prison for robbing banks. Now, that's the kind of thing country songs are made of."

Luke laughed. "That's me, a walkin' country song."

"What was your musical influence?"

"Hell, I don't know. I think it was born in me. My mom played piano and guitar, my brother Bobby played piano, and I had some aunts and uncles that played, so music was common in our house. My first music memory is Jimmie Rodgers on an old wind-up Victrola. My mom said that before I could talk, I would try to yodel like Jimmie Rodgers."

"I'm a huge Jimmie Rodgers fan. Woody Guthrie, too."

The two men seemed oblivious of the women as they continued. Luke stood and put his guitar back on the stand. "I'm about ready for a Beam and Coke. Want one, Frank?"

"No, this beer is fine for me. But, I hope you aren't done playing. I'd like to hear more."

He noticed Darlina putting the final touches on a sandwich tray. "Let's eat a bite and I'll play some more. Do you play, Frank?"

"Nah. I can play the radio real good. I am what you'd call a true lover of music."

"Come on, you guys." Darlina called from the kitchen.

Frank followed Judy into the dining room and the four sat around the long table.

Conversation continued while they ate.

"You know, when I first got to Leavenworth, I was mad, bitter and rebellious. I knew I hadn't done what I'd been convicted of and I was gonna to show 'em how pissed I was." Luke paused to take a bite. "It took over three years for me to figure out I wasn't big enough or bad enough to change prison. I cursed music and blamed the lifestyle that went with it for the predicament I was in. But, it was my own ignorance and arrogance that landed me there, not the music."

Judy reached for the pickle jar. "Me and Roxy were living in New Mexico when we heard of Luke's arrest. We couldn't believe it. We'd followed his music since we were kids in high school. We even saw him and Dean Beard walking down the street one day in Coleman, but were too shy to approach them."

"I can't imagine you being shy, Judy," Frank teased.

"Like I said, we were just kids. I got over being shy. Roxy never did."

"Judy tells me you played with some of the greatest artists of our time. Willie Nelson, Bob Wills, Bobby Bare, Red Foley?"

"It's true. I played with all of 'em. I'll never forget the day my booking agent, Sam Gibbs, called me from Wichita Falls and said Bob Wills needed a band to back him and would I be interested. It was right after Bob had sold the Texas Playboys name. I didn't ask how much the gig paid or anything else. I just said, when and where? Playing with Bob Wills was the highlight of my life. We were booked as Bob Wills and the Boys. I'd love to run across one of those old posters." He reached across the table for Darlina's hand. "The other highlight was meeting this little girl."

He noticed Darlina blush.

She fidgeted. "I was a young girl when I met Luke, only nineteen, and fresh away from a holy-roller home. I had no idea about life, but I was ready and anxious to try it all."

Luke leaned back and wiped his mouth. "She was go-go dancing in an after-hours club that had lost its liquor license for serving to minors. I thought she was about the prettiest little thing I'd ever seen with her long legs, blue eyes, auburn hair and sexy little ass." He grinned and winked. "Still do."

Darlina picked up the story. "I hung out at that club because I wasn't old enough to get into the real ones. Then the owner, a lady from Czechoslovakia, took me under her wing, taught me how to dance and let me wait tables for tips. I loved live music and bands played there every weekend. When Luke and his band came in one night to eat, the whole place stirred. I was curious and traded with another gal to wait their table." She flashed Luke a smile. "The rest is history."

"Well, you two seem like a story-book couple. I'm envious. I've been married a couple of times, but can't really say I loved either of them. I just got in heat." Frank pushed his chair back.

"Oh, we're just like everyone else. We don't always see eye-to-eye, and especially when we were raising our girls. Darlina thought I was too hard on them and I thought she was too soft." Luke took a swig from his glass.

"Still, we never stopped loving each other no matter what." Darlina finished the sentence. "We waited too long and went through too much to let anything destroy us."

Judy nodded. "Frank, besides me and Roxy, these two love each other more than anyone I know. And, I wish we had time, I'd love for you to see their antique store next door. You saw the Saturday Store when we drove up. Some of Grandma's dishes are on consignment in it."

"I do love antique stores, but that will have to be another visit." He turned back to Luke. "Were you guys married before you went to prison, Luke?" Frank finished his beer.

"No. In fact, I was still married to my second wife when I met Darlina. I hadn't lived with her in years. We couldn't get along at all, but we had a mess of kids and I supported them. Until Darlina came along, I had no reason to think about a divorce. By then, it was too late."

"What do you mean?"

"I was already knee-deep in the shit that sent me to prison, so I figured the only honorable thing I could do was get Darlina away from me and out of what was coming down."

"So, he said ugly things and told me it had been fun, but he was tired of a kid. He needed a real woman." Darlina's voice faded.

"I hated like hell to do it, but that was the only way I could get her to go away. She didn't deserve to be caught in the middle of that shit."

"Of course, I didn't know it at the time. I just thought he didn't love me anymore. I'd have gone to the ends of the earth with him."

Luke continued. "I knew that and my conscience couldn't let that happen. We got married a week after I got paroled."

"Wow! That's quite a story. You guys ought to write a book."

"Nobody would believe it if we did." Luke stood. "Let's go back to the living room."

"I'll help Darlina clean up." Judy pushed her chair back.

"How about another beer, Frank? Judy?" Darlina stacked plates.

"I'll get it." Judy carried an armful of dishes to the sink.

Back in the living room, Luke sat his whiskey down and reached for the guitar. He played Wynn Stewart songs, Marty Robbins ballads, Ned Miller tunes and wound it down with an old Jimmie Rodgers standard.

When he wiped the guitar down and put it in the case, Frank pushed his lanky frame up from the chair. "We'd better be going, Judy. I've got a long drive tomorrow."

Luke stood and slapped him on the back. "It was great to meet you. Hope I didn't bore you too much with my tall tales."

"Oh hell no. I'd love to hear more, but, I'm driving on to New Mexico tomorrow."

Luke hugged Judy.

"Well, if you're ever back this way, stop in."

"That I will do."

"Bye, you guys." Darlina and Luke stood under the carport until they backed out of the driveway.

"That was unexpected." Luke closed and locked the door.

"Sweetheart, I think you better get ready because folks are going to start coming out of the woodwork when they hear you're playing again."

He pulled her into a crushing embrace and buried his face in her hair. "I love the opportunity to tell everyone I meet what an angel you are. I don't mean to embarrass you, I just want 'em to know."

Darlina raised her head. "I suppose we do have a story that people find unusual. To us, it's just the way our lives went."

"I don't know many women who would've stood by a worn out, broke down convict musician for so many long years, holding on to a dream. But, that's what you did, and your dream kept me going when I had no other reason in the world."

Darlina sighed against his chest. "It kept me going too. All I ever wanted was to be your wife. It just took a long time to get there."

"Everything I am, everything I have, is all for and because of you, princess. Don't ever forget that. If I die tonight, I'd have no complaints."

"Well, if you die tonight, I'll have lots of complaints, so let's don't even talk like that."

The two walked arm-in-arm through the rooms, turning out the lights.

"You know the sand in my hourglass is going to run out one of these days, baby," Luke murmured.

"Then we'll face it when that day comes, but today isn't it." Darlina pressed her slender body against his.

"No, today isn't the day."

Chapter 2

"Dammit!" Luke eased himself down from the last rung on the ladder as the muscle in his left leg tightened in an uncontrollable spasm. He hobbled to an overturned bucket and sat down, rubbing the calf of the leg.

Just then Darlina rounded the corner of the trailer. "Honey, what's wrong?" she called out, walking toward him.

"These damned leg cramps are getting worse and now I'm having them in the daytime too," he growled. "When's my next appointment with Dr. Robertson?"

"Next week. Think I should try to get you in sooner?" She squatted beside the bucket and took over massaging the convulsing muscle.

Luke put a hand on her shoulder. "No. I think I can hold out, but something's gotta be done. I've tried everything I know and so have you."

She looked up. "We'll figure it out, baby. Maybe Dr. Robert-son will have some answers."

"Maybe so. You know it's killing me to not be able to make love the way you need it."

She looked up at him. "Maybe it isn't you, Luke."

"How could you even think that? I want and need you as much as I ever did. I'm damned frustrated." He focused on a bee buzzing around a newly opened rose bud.

Darlina stood. "It's time to talk to the doctor about it." He didn't miss the hurt in her eyes.

"Gotta get back to work." Luke spat, and climbed back up the ladder.

His chest tightened as he watched her walk through the back door of their antique store. How could she possibly think he didn't want her anymore? Hadn't he done everything in his power to show her? His body wasn't cooperating. Perhaps this was the price to pay for getting old. At any rate, it crushed him and there had to be a solution. One thing he wouldn't or couldn't do was stop trying.

***

A few days later, Dr. Robertson, Luke's cardiovascular doctor, ordered a Doppler scan on the lower extremities after examining him and listening to his complaints.

Luke knew he couldn't expect to feel like a young man. And maybe the doctor was on to something. Perhaps it was directly related to poor circulation. Dr. Robertson agreed it would explain the excruciating leg cramps, which caused Luke to walk the floor for hours on end. He also explained that without proper blood flow, sex would be more difficult.

It was time for some answers and solutions.

He and Darlina sat in the doctor's office, two weeks later, to hear the results of the test.

"Mr. Stone, the test shows what I suspected. This is all part of the atherosclerosis that you suffer from. The main artery on the left side of your lower extremity is 90% blocked. The right is only 45% blocked, so our focus is on the left side." Dr. Robertson studied the report in front of him.

"Oh hell! What can we do, Doc?" Luke dared a glance at Darlina. Would this mean another surgery? Dread filled him at the thought.

"I'm going to recommend what we call a Fem-Popliteal Bypass graft. What that means in plain English is that we'll take part of an artery out of your arm and use it to bypass the blockage in the affected area."

"Shit, that sounds painful. How long will something like that lay me up? I've got work orders to fill. " Luke's frown deepened.

"You'll be hospitalized for a few days. Then of course, there will be a recovery period where you'll need to limit activity."

Luke turned to Darlina. "Here we go again, honey. I'm so sorry."

Her blue eyes stared at him. "Oh Luke, please don't say that. There's nothing to apologize for."

"I can apologize for being a broken down old man, but nothing much I can do to change it."

Dr. Robertson peered over the top rim of his glasses. "I don't want to hear you talk like that. You're still a young man compared to the average life span nowadays. You've got lots of living ahead of you. I do, however, highly recommend that you keep your diet low fat and cut the amount of whiskey you're drinking in half. I've suggested to you before that you drink a glass of red wine every day."

"I know, Doc, but I just can't stand the taste of it. I guess if you think it'll help, I'll find a way to get it down." Luke set his mouth.

Darlina glanced up at the doctor. "I had him on a strict low fat diet, but we've kinda gotten away from it. I still have all of my recipes and it'll be easy to pull them back out."

"Shit, Doc. Don't put me on lettuce and carrots." Luke fidgeted on the chair. "I don't do rabbit food. I can quit the whiskey. I've quit everything in life that I needed to."

Dr. Robertson laughed and slapped Luke on the knee. "Don't worry. It won't be just lettuce and carrots. You do need to cut down on red meat and fried foods. That's a starting place."

Luke grumbled. "Might as well just go ahead and shoot me like they do a lame horse."

"Don't pay any attention to him, Dr. Robertson. He'll adjust," Darlina assured the physician.

"Yeah, well I can tell you right now I ain't eatin' none of that damned processed turkey. They burned me out on that shit when I was in prison." Luke grimaced.

Dr. Robertson chuckled and stood. "I'll write the order for the hospital and you can talk with my nurse, Becky, before you leave. She'll give you all of the details."

Luke extended his hand. "Thanks again, Doc."

By the time they left the office that day, Luke had an appointment on June 19th for the procedure.

He watched Darlina out of the corner of his eye as she signed papers, presented the insurance card and chatted with Becky.

She did so much and never complained about hard work or his many shortcomings.

She was his princess in every way. Once again, he was left with the longing to do more and to give her the world on a silver platter.

In his opinion, there had never been anyone more deserving. He would do whatever it took, even if it meant eating lettuce and carrots to stay with her as long as he possibly could.

*****

So, two weeks later, Luke found himself holding a hated backless hospital gown in preparation for more surgery.

"Sugar, maybe this'll be the last time around for more hospital shit," he said once the nurses left the room. "Hell, my ol' body's starting to look like a Texas roadmap from all the scars."

She helped him out of his clothes and into the gown. "We can always hope."

He grabbed her hand when she reached around him for the tie that had escaped. "Sweetheart, I couldn't do any of this without you. You know that don't you?" He kissed her slender fingers.

"All I know is that you'll never have to, because I'm not going anywhere." She finished tying the gown then kissed him on the back of the neck.

Luke sighed. "I ain't ready to throw in the towel yet."

She smiled. "And neither am I, so we'll just keep on keepin' on. I'm so glad we took that trip to Mexico with Sally and Jim when we did."

"You're not ever gonna let me live that one down, are you?" Luke settled back on the narrow hospital bed.

"Nope." He didn't miss the twinkle in her eyes. "I know you thought Sally and I had gone behind your back to plan the trip without consulting you, but that simply wasn't true. And look at what an amazing time we had and how close you and Jim got during that time."

"Yes. I can admit when I'm wrong. I was wrong, dammit. Happy?"

Her laugh tinkled. "As a matter of fact I am, but I'll be happier when this procedure is over and we get you back home, on your feet and making love to me again."

He grew serious. "Me too, darlin'."

He moved over and patted the bed beside him. With her head lying gently on his chest, he stroked her hair and allowed his thoughts to roam freely. They turned to his friend, Jim, and the battle he was facing with lung cancer.

When he spoke, his words faltered. "I've lost too many spirit brothers lately and I'm afraid Jim isn't going to be here for long."

Darlina pushed herself up and looked into his eyes. "I hope you're wrong, for Sally's sake, if nothing else."

"So do I," he sighed. "I don't talk much about it, but I often wonder what in the hell ever happened to my ol' podnah, Red Hoss. We were as close as any two brothers."

"I know. I wonder about him too. I always felt indebted to Red. Remember Christmas Eve, 1970?"

Luke nodded. "Well, I remember what I was told."

"I couldn't stand to see you thrashing around on the bed with such a high fever. I wanted to take you to the hospital, but Red said no. I was so young and scared. You kept ranting about the civil war and agonizing about your leg being cut off on the battlefield." She looked away. "That was my first introduction to past lives and you made a believer out of me."

"Those experiences were as real as this backless gown and hard-assed hospital bed." Luke reached for an extra pillow and pushed it under his head. "They stopped when I went to prison. I couldn't afford to let myself be vulnerable at any cost in there."

"I used to think about it, but I knew Red would help you if it happened again. Do you think he's dead?"

"My gut tells me he isn't. Guess I'll never know for sure." Luke's voice trailed off.

"You've done all you can to find him. And Jim's taking the chemo trying to hang on. He and Sally are doing a lot of living in the meantime. That's what we have to do, too."

"I damned well intend to." He brought Darlina's fingertips to his lips.

Darlina kissed Luke and stood straightening the sheet around him. "Sally and Jim are a lot like us in that they got a second chance at love."

"The fickle finger of fate." Luke laughed. "Oh how my brother, Bobby, used to love that phrase. Well, I hope they get that damned cancer in remission so they can have lots more years together. They're true friends."

Two nurses entered and interrupted the conversation. "Mr. Stone," the older one said, "we need to shave and prep you for surgery."

"I reckon that's what I'm here for. Do whatever you need to."

Darlina moved aside to allow the nurses to do their job.

Luke made every effort to remain lighthearted and joked with the nurses as they shaved the entire length of his left leg and arm.

"Here's one I used to tell my little girls that always made 'em laugh. Know what the duck said when he ordered soup at the diner?"

The nurse giggled. "No, what?"

"Got any quackers?"

Both nurses chuckled. "You've at least got a sense of humor, sir."

"Figure that's the best way to handle any of this hospital stuff. None of us want to be here and no need in being grouchy."

"We wish all of our patients had that attitude." The nurse laid the razor in a tray and they proceeded to clean up. Once finished, they asked if Luke needed anything and left the room.

"Honey, would you slide that tray over here so I can reach the remote?"

Darlina positioned the tray then sat back on the side of the bed and held Luke's hand. "I feel good about this procedure, baby."

Luke stroked her hand. "Me too, but as always if something breaks bad, just know how much I love you and I always will." He pulled her to his chest.

"I love you too, sweetheart," she murmured.

***

Just as Dr. Robertson had predicted, Luke spent four days in the hospital. Darlina never left his side and the surgery appeared to be a success.

When Dr. Robertson presented the results of the new Doppler test showing a significant increase of blood flow in the previously blocked area, once again, it seemed Luke had been given another chance at the quality of life he desired. Her hopes soared that he would be her husband in every way again. She knew the blow his ego took when he had difficulty functioning sexually.

It went against everything he represented as a man. And even though he'd reassured her many times it had nothing to do with her, she still couldn't shake the doubt that maybe she didn't turn him on anymore. Time would tell.

She packed up their things in preparation to return home, while half-listening to a story Luke told the male nurse who prepared to escort him to the car.

It struck her how Luke had the ability to engage with everyone he met. She'd never realized this was a true gift.

Darlina drove as they headed back to Coleman. She noticed that Luke gingerly sat to the right side to take pressure off of the left.

"Baby, I'm trying to avoid as many bumps in the road as possible."

He laid a hand on her knee. "I know you are, honey. I'm sore as hell, but that's to be expected. I'll be okay in a few days. And when I get back on my feet, I'm going to show you just how much I love you."

Darlina giggled. "I can't wait for that part. Are you sure you aren't tired of me, Luke? Maybe you need a younger, more beautiful woman."

Luke sighed. "Oh hell! I don't know how many ways I can say it. I want and need only you and it's time you got it through your stubborn head."

"Okay. Don't get mad. I just have to ask. I have my own insecurities from time to time, you know."

"Well, you haven't got a damned thing to be insecure about," he growled. After a few minutes of silence, he glanced back at her. "I don't know how many chances a man gets in life, but I've had more than my fair share. I'm like a cat with nine lives and I've quit counting 'cause I don't want 'em to end."

"You keep getting chances because you try to stay positive and always move forward instead of backward. I believe that's what keeps good things happening for you, for us."

"Maybe." Luke stared out the window. "I learned in prison that the only way to make it through life is to be positive. I had hell learning that, though, and it damned near killed me. It's not always easy, but it always works. Thank you for sticking with me, sugar."

Darlina spared a glance. "There's no place I'd rather be, Luke Stone."

She intertwined her fingers in his as the miles clicked off. It was true. She couldn't think of anywhere she'd rather be than next to Luke. As far as she was concerned, she was born to be Luke's partner and she would let nothing change that.

Luke, Sally, Darlina and Jim in a Cantina in Mexico

Chapter 3

O nce they made it home, Darlina offered her arm for Luke to lean on as he hobbled into the house to his easy chair.

"Sweetheart, you just take it easy and I'll get our things out of the car, but first I'm going to fix you a fresh glass of tea." Darlina moved to the kitchen.

"Honey, do you think you could go out to the sign shop and check things out for me? Just make sure everything is still intact."

"Of course. I want to look in on The Saturday store too." Darlina put the water on to boil for tea. "I'll be back in a minute."

She glanced at Luke when she brought their bags in from the car and was relieved to see that he'd dozed off. He needed to rest. She felt sure he'd be up and around within a few days.

With tea bags steeping in the hot water, she quietly closed the door, went to gather the mail and check on the businesses.

Funny, how she always got a little excited every time she went into the Saturday Store. With so many quality antiques and the shelves full of shiny collectables, she couldn't help having a sense of accomplishment.

She remembered how it had come to Luke in a dream a couple of years after his mother had passed on. He'd seen a sign hanging in front of the empty house that read *The Saturday Store*.

As with everything that Luke and Darlina did, bit-by-bit, they'd built the business into a thriving little store to be proud of.

Now, as she walked through, she marveled at the many items they'd stocked on the shelves.

Then, she hurried on to the sign shop, and back to the trailer to keep an eye on Luke and start a load of laundry.

She had work to do and part of that included getting out all of the recipes she'd worked so hard creating not long after Dr. Robertson had sent Luke to Lubbock to be evaluated for a heart transplant a few years back. It was time to get on track with the diet. Anything she could do to keep Luke healthy was effort worth making.

Later that evening, as she sat with Luke watching a country music show on TV, the phone rang. She hurried to answer it.

"Hello."

"Hi, Darlina." Sally's voice came through the line. "Jim and I wanted to check on Luke and say hi. Today's Jim's birthday and we've been celebrating. We even had birthday sex."

Darlina giggled. "Birthday sex is the best." She glanced at Luke to see him grinning broadly. "Luke's doing good. We got home today and he's taking it easy. Here, I'll put him on. I know he wants to talk to Jim."

Darlina handed the phone to Luke and listened to his end of the conversation.

She laughed as Luke joked with his friend about birthday sex and then made it around to asking about his health. Luke's face grew solemn.

Finally, he said. "Well man, you know if there's anything we can do we will. We need to get together again soon."

After another pause, Luke wrapped up the conversation. "Yeah, she's right here. I know she wants to wish you happy birthday. You hang in there podnah and let me know if you need anything."

He handed the phone back to Darlina. She wished Jim a happy birthday, and then hung up.

"What did he say?" She saw sadness in Luke's eyes.

"He said he didn't think he'd be around much longer and the pain is almost unbearable at times."

"My heart goes out to Sally." She moved back to her chair next to Luke. "I can't even think about how lost she's going to be." Tears clogged her throat. Damn! She hated death.

Luke sighed. "Life is such a funny thing. I've always related it to the seasons and the trees. In the spring, the leaves come on the trees all fresh and vibrant, then flourish through the summer only to turn brilliant hues of brown and orange in the fall. Then they drop from the trees leaving them barren. It's the same with the cycle of life and death."

"I just don't know how I could go on living if I lost you." She looked down at her hands folded on her lap.

"Come over here, darlin'." Luke patted the arm of his chair.

She sat down beside him and he put his arm around her waist, pulling her close. She kissed his cheek. "I love you."

Luke turned to look into her eyes. "I know, baby, and I can't figure how on earth I got so lucky, but I did and you are my angel." He kissed her parted lips.

It amazed her how their closeness only grew with the passing of time.

Ironically, it seemed that each loss in life drew them more in-tune, more in-sync and more aligned with one other.

Perhaps it was how the yin-yang, good-bad, up-down worked.

***

A few short weeks later, Luke and Darlina received word from Sally that they'd called in Hospice and Jim asked to speak to Luke one last time.

By the end of the conversation with Sally and Jim that night, both Luke and Darlina knew they'd had their last conversation with Jim on this earth.

"Honey, would you get the jar with the Sweetgrass in it? I want to burn some for Jim and light a candle too." the somber look on Luke's face put her in motion. "I know it's strange, but this is part of my American Indian religion, to offer up smoke in ceremony."

She walked to the den and took the jar from the shelf, then went to the kitchen for matches. After she lit a candle, she handed both the Sweetgrass and matches to Luke and watched as he stood and did sacred ceremony for his brother in spirit who was preparing to make the crossing.

Voice choking with emotion, he began. "I call upon the Great Spirit to guide my brother, Jim, through the pain that this world inflicts. May he cross between the worlds with ease and with grace. Until we meet again." He waved the smoke that swirled upward from the Sweetgrass in the four directions, then handed it to Darlina and sat back in his chair.

She laid the still smoldering braid of Sweetgrass in a pan and joined Luke. She cradled her head softly against his. She didn't feel the need to hold back the tears that silently made their way down her cheeks.

Words were not necessary.

***

Later that night, Luke lay panting beside Darlina on their antique iron bed. A grin began to form and grew broader and broader.

He turned on his side toward her. "Now, do you still feel like there's something wrong with you and I don't find you attractive anymore?"

Her grin matched his. "No, I guess I don't. That was just like we used to make love and maybe even better." She touched his face with tears misting her eyes.

"Ah, now, don't you start crying on me. You should be happy."

She sniffed. "I am. It's just that I feel so much love my heart may burst open."

"Come here," he said gruffly and pulled her close. "My ol' ticker's about to jump right out of my chest. Can you hear it?"

She nodded.

"Don't ever doubt yourself, angel. You're beautiful and warm and sweet and the best of everything I could ever have dreamed up. Get it through your hard head that I love you and no one else and I need you and no one else."

She raised her head to gaze into his clear blue eyes. "Me too, baby. Me too."

Luke held her tight. He had his life back one more time. He silently gave thanks to the Great Spirit as he stroked her silky hair. A deep sigh escaped and he branded the fresh memory of their passion deep into his brain. If a drought came again, he'd have the memories and nothing would take them.

Chapter 4

L uke wasn't the kind of man to get excited about much of anything. Life had pitched too many disappointments his way to put much stock in any one event.

All the same, the phone call he received a few days later started his heart to racing just a little.

Sometimes life had a way of throwing surprises and opportunities your direction that you could not see coming, as was the case with this unexpected phone call. It seemed that a reporter had gotten wind of Luke's story through friends of Roxy Gordon and wanted to do a magazine article about him. Although he couldn't guarantee it, the man was hopeful he could sell the piece to Texas Monthly Magazine, the most widely distributed magazine in the state.

Anxious to tell Darlina, Luke wondered if he should call her at work or wait until she came home for lunch. One glance at the clock told him it was less than an hour until lunch. He could wait.

As he expertly eased his paint brush along the edges of the letters on a new sign, his thoughts turned to their oldest daughter, Lily, and the engagement announcement she'd made a few months ago. Almost as if by magic, the jingling of the phone brought him back.

"Hello." He balanced the paint brush on the table's edge.

"Hi, Dad. You busy?" Lily's familiar voice tugged at his heart.

"Never too busy for you, sweetheart. What's up?"

"I just wanted to tell you and Mom that Alexander and I have found the church we are going to be married in and set a date in November. I wanted to ask if you'd walk me down the aisle."

"Of course, if that's what you want, sugar. But, what about Will? He's your biological father."

"As far as I'm concerned, you're my dad. Will has never shown any interest in my life and I'm sure he wouldn't start now. I want you to give me away."

"Honey, you know I'd like nothing better. Tell me about the church."

Lily described a historic church in downtown Dallas and even though he was happy for her, a twinge of sadness washed over him. He was getting old and his girls were all grown up. He wished for an instant that he could turn back the hands of time. Back to when the girls still loved to sit on his lap, back to when he was still young enough to build a new life.

He talked with Lily for a few more minutes, shared the news about the pending interview, and then held the phone a second longer than her goodbye.

His chest swelled with pride. Lily wanted him to walk her down the aisle. He couldn't think of a greater honor. He only hoped the man who was lucky enough to have her would always treat her with care and respect. If not, he'd have to answer to him, that much he knew.

Glancing back at the clock, he dropped the paint brush into a can of Acetone and headed to the house.

From the refrigerator he chose fat-free bologna for himself and turkey breast for Darlina. She'd changed a lot about the foods he ate and he did his best to go along with all of it, but prison had ruined him where processed turkey was concerned. He grabbed the loaf of reduced fat whole wheat bread and went to work.

He thought about the routines they'd fallen into. Every day Darlina came home from work, fixed lunch for them, looked at the mail and talked to Luke until it was time to go back.

In prison, he'd hated routines, but theirs was different, even comforting in a deep way.

***

The minute she walked into the coolness of the house on the blazing August day, Darlina immediately knew something was up. Maybe it was the gleam in Luke's eyes, or maybe it was the lunch already spread out on the table. At any rate, she knew.

"Hello, sweetheart." She stood on her tiptoes to receive his kiss. "You fixed lunch."

"I thought it was time I did something nice for you. Besides I have some news that I want to tell you and didn't want to have to wait another minute."

"What's going on?" She sat down in the chair Luke pulled out for her.

He settled into his chair before he continued. "I got a phone call today. A man named Josh Alan Friedman says he's a writer and reporter. Roxy's friends, Bob and Sally Ackerman, told him about me and he wants to do an interview. He's pretty sure he can sell the story to *Texas Monthly Magazine*, but knows without a doubt he can get it published in *No Depression*."

"Oh my God! That's wonderful." Darlina pushed her chair back and threw her arms around Luke's neck. "How can you sit there so calm? Did he say what questions he might ask?"

His crooked grin that always melted her heart formed instantly. "Well, he mentioned the bank robberies and said the Ackermans told him about me singing at Roxy's memorial and how it had been thirty years since I'd performed in public. He said he finds the story interesting."

"Of course he does. Everyone does, but to get into Texas Monthly? That is huge, baby." As she moved back to her chair, tingles raced up and down her spine.

"You're telling me. You know I hardly ever get excited about anything, but this got me stirred up. If nothing else, a bunch of people that might be wondering if I'm still alive will not have to wonder anymore." Luke chuckled.

"When does the reporter want to do this interview?" Darlina bit into her sandwich.

"In a couple of weeks, but he'll call when he has a date."

"This could help bring more business into our little store and who knows, maybe even some music opportunities."

"I've sat here and worked my ass off for fifteen years and been happy to do it, but damn if it doesn't seem like it's time for a break. That's not my only news today."

"Oh my lord, Luke, what else? I've only been gone four hours." She reached for a napkin.

"Lily called this morning. She said her and Alexander have found the church they want to be married in and she wanted to know if I'd walk her down the aisle."

Darlina looked up, tears misting her eyes. "Oh honey, I know how much that means to you. Then again, you are her dad, so why wouldn't she ask you?"

"Well, I thought she might want Will to do it, but she let me know that wasn't anything she'd consider. Our girls are all grown up, graduated from college and Nicole's gone off to law school way up in Colorado. I'm very proud of them, but it all happened too fast." He reached across the table and dabbed Darlina's eyes with his napkin. "Don't cry, sweetheart. You'll ruin your makeup."

Darlina smiled through her tears. "We have a lot to be thankful for and a hell of a lot to be proud of and these are happy tears."

Luke laid a calloused hand across hers. "Why don't we invite Judy in for supper tonight and we can share this news with her. I feel so sorry for her."

"I agree. Will you call her?"

Luke nodded.

The two sat at the small table and finished lunch while continuing to talk about the prospect of this interview, Lily's wedding and Nicole's brave venture.

On the way back to work, Darlina could feel excitement coursing through her. Somehow, she sensed this would be good for Luke and what was good for him was wonderful for her. She couldn't wait to share this news with her good friend, Elora. Over the years at the same job, Darlina had established many friendships, but the one with Elora went beyond, to something more like sisterhood. It was Elora who covered her workload when she had to be away due to Luke's hospitalizations. It was Elora she could count on to listen to anything she had to say without judgment. And, Darlina, in turn, did the same for her. Between Elora and Sally, she had two friends who would always stand beside and support her and Luke.

When Luke had gotten back on stage for the first time in thirty years, Darlina couldn't have been more proud and she loved sharing that epic moment with her friends. It wasn't easy for Luke, and he'd been overly concerned about looking and sounding like an old man.

Nothing she said could convince him that he didn't. It would take someone other than herself. Maybe this interview would provide the boost he needed.

Now that he played his guitar daily and had even written some new songs, Darlina knew this fulfilled his life purpose. Without it, he wasn't complete. He'd mentioned that he might start booking some shows and that thrilled her even more.

Bursting at the seams to share this latest news with her friend, Darlina made a beeline for Elora's office the minute she walked through the door.

***

Mid-August, shortly after Luke's sixty-fifth birthday, Josh Alan Friedman arrived in Coleman for a day of interviewing.

Happy that Darlina took the day off work, Luke let her know that her presence gave him confidence.

He sized up the man seated across from them. Josh Alan was tall with a thick shock of dark hair, dark glasses and a large nose. He wore a black t-shirt and jeans, and looked as if he could fight his way out of any situation. He had a strong Brooklyn accent and Luke immediately liked his direct way of speaking.

After a few minutes of polite conversation, Luke began to open up and the story flowed out of him. How he'd been a singing star back in the day, naming the many artists he'd worked with. He lingered a while on the time period of working with Bob Wills and expressed how much he loved the man.

He talked about how he was at the beginning of the Outlaw music movement before it had a name. He told how he could draw hippies out of Georgetown and cowboys out of Round Rock with his brand of music, and there were never any problems.

Then he told about getting mixed up with some men who were robbing banks during a time when he didn't think he cared about much of anything in life anymore. He stressed to the reporter that he'd never gone into a bank with a gun and robbed it, but because he wouldn't rat and tell what he knew, they gave him two armed robbery convictions.

During the course of the morning, Luke gave the reporter a full tour of their property, pointing out each improvement. He glowed with pride when Darlina explained how hard it had been inching their way forward from nothing.

He ushered Josh Alan into the back room of the house next door, which they'd acquired a few years ago. Luke had turned it into a music museum of sorts by hanging pictures of the many artists he'd worked with, on the walls, along with promotional pictures of him and his band.

Josh examined an elaborate turntable system with speakers suspended from the ceiling. The cassette, eight track and reel-to-reel players got his attention as well. But, the fully functioning wire recorder piqued his curiosity the most. Luke could fill the room with music from most any era.

They moved into the adjoining rooms, which held a growing collection of vinyl records that now numbered close to ten thousand.

Back at the trailer, Luke proudly showed off his and Darlina's recently remodeled bedroom with gold embossed wallpaper, red carpet and red satin bedspread while Darlina went to a local steak house to bring back lunch.

Once they'd eaten, the three gathered in the den and Luke recounted the trip to the heart doctor in Lubbock a few years back. He couldn't help noticing the way Darlina's eyes took on a troubled look.

He explained how Dr. Robertson had sent him to be evaluated for a heart transplant in 1996 because of the weakened condition of the heart muscle. The Lubbock cardiologist had informed Luke that he was not a candidate for a transplant due to the nature of his disease. He advised him to go back home, eat nothing but beans, rice and pasta and he might live another six months.

He chuckled. "I told Darlina on the way home that I'd die when I got damned good and ready and I wasn't ready. Of course, she was all upset and crying." He paused to reach for her hand. "But after we got home, this wife of mine went to work and put together a diet for me. I mean she spent countless hours with nutrition books, analyzing and breaking down every food. Then she figured out ways to fix things I like without 'em being unhealthy. And yes, I know I just ate a steak, but that's a pretty rare occasion anymore."

Darlina smiled at Josh Alan. "He exaggerates. I only did what anyone would do in the same situation. But, I put him on an extremely low fat diet and he immediately dropped over forty pounds. He kept it off for several years. We've recently gotten back on the diet."

Finally, Josh Alan stood and stretched. "Man, I've got to get back to Dallas. I think you've given me plenty to work with. I'll be in touch when I have something."

"It's been a pleasure to talk to you. Thank you for the autographed copy of your book, *Tales of Times Square*. I look forward to reading it. Come back anytime." Luke stood and extended his hand. Darlina joined him.

"I promise I'll return for a visit."

After the reporter left, Luke pulled Darlina close to his side. "Honey, we may not have much, but lots of folks seem to be fascinated by what we've managed to do."

"I meant it when I told Josh Alan your biggest talent was taking nothing and making something amazing from it. Well, that and of course, making music." She nestled her head into Luke's shoulder.

"And I meant it when I told him that everything I do is for you." He kissed the top of her head.

"I never get tired of holding you, baby." His hand slipped to her bottom.

"In spite of everything, we've managed to build a pretty good life, haven't we? Do you have any regrets?" He felt her hands slide down his back like tender butterfly touches.

"Only that I wasted too many damn years being stupid. How about you?"

"No regrets."

"No wishing for a younger man?"

"Nope."

Luke brought his hands up to her face and tilted it. Her lips parted to receive his kiss that lasted a long moment in time and sent shivers up and down his spine.

Finally, he came up for air.

Chapter 5

A few days later, Darlina came home from work to find that they had company. Curious as to whom it might be, she hurried into the house.

When she opened the door, she was met with the ringing of the Martin D-35 and Luke's smooth baritone. The minute he saw her, he stopped playing and she leaned to kiss him.

"Honey, this is my old uncle, Claude. I know you've heard me talk about him."

With a smile, Darlina turned to the man and woman seated on the sofa. She stretched out her hand. Instead of taking it, Claude rose and caught her in a bear hug.

Claude stood over six feet and had a thick neck that melded into his shoulders. His ruddy complexion and sparse hair reminded her of a stereotypical Irishman. She remembered stories about him playing football in his younger days and then playing on the pro golf circuit. "It is so nice to finally get to meet you, Claude."

"And it's nice to meet you. I admire the woman who can tame my wild-ass nephew." The woman who sat beside him stood. "This is my wife, Hilda," Claude said.

Darlina hugged her. "Welcome to our home. I hope you'll be staying for dinner."

"Now, we don't want to be any trouble," Claude boomed. "I just wanted to see Luke and catch up. I've been out of the country over in Norway for a long time."

Darlina saw through Claude's rough exterior. And Hilda was a very pretty woman with flashing brown eyes and a quick smile. "It won't be any trouble. I'd love it if you'd stay. I'm glad that you got Luke to play and sing for you." Darlina placed a hand on Luke's shoulder.

"Hell, honey, Claude threatened to break my arm if I didn't." Luke chuckled.

Darlina winked. "Good tactic, Claude. Y'all go ahead with your visiting. I'm gonna change out of my work clothes and whip us up some supper."

"I'll be happy to help." Hilda spoke with a lilting Norwegian accent.

"Sure. That'd be great." Darlina headed to the bedroom. She thought of the time Luke had admonished her for trying to do everything herself and not letting anyone help. She'd welcome Hilda's help and it would give Luke and Claude more time to visit.

Luke had told her stories of how Claude broke him into the oilfield at the age of sixteen. He said it was Claude who'd made him tough, making fun of him when he got sick from his first cigarette; taunting him and calling him sister when he hesitated to grab onto heavy tongs on the oil rig. In truth, Claude had helped make Luke the man he was and had instilled in him a fierce drive to excel.

She hurried back to their company, but not before grabbing a package of frozen barbeque brisket from the freezer and putting it in warm water to thaw.

Darlina had learned along the way that having things in the freezer already cooked and packaged made life easier when company dropped in unexpectedly, as they so often did these days.

Just as she walked back into the room, she heard Luke laughing at Claude's story.

"Remember when we worked on that rig out of Odessa and the prostitutes would come out after dark?" Claude pointed his finger at Luke.

"Hell yeah, I remember. You know, Claude, that was a time when oil rigs stretched for miles on end. I'll never forget how those lights shone at night like diamonds, and as far as the eye could see."

Claude shook his head. "Shit, a man could quit one job and have another that paid twenty cents more an hour before the sweat dried on his brow. Things sure have changed. Hey, I've got some cold beer out in the pickup." He turned to his wife. "Hilda, go get some of those cold beers. Want one, Luke?"

"Nah. I stick with that old Jim Beam. I haven't had a beer in thirty or more years."

"Well, then, go get some for me and you, Hilda."

Hilda stood and reached for the keys. "I'll be right back. Darlina, do you want one?"

"No thanks. Luke, would you like for me to fix you a drink?"

"I'd love that, honey." He winked at her when she walked past him.

When she returned with the beverage, she pulled up a chair and listened as the two men told their stories. She compared physical similarities between the men. Luke was a large man, like Claude, but taller and thinner with a darker complexion and silver-gray hair.

Claude had opted for overseas work and met Hilda in Norway. Even though Claude spoke in a gruff voice to his wife, the love the two shared was evident. It seemed that Claude spoke to everyone in a gruff voice. That was simply his way.

"Hey, Luke, we're coming back to Coleman in October for the high school reunion. You oughta come out and see everyone."

"Hell, man, nobody would want to see me. Besides that, remember, I didn't graduate. I still had half a year left when I decided I was too grown up for school and headed to the patch."

"Just the same, we should have a get-together. Living down on the coast, I can catch all the fish in the world. And I've got a fish cooker I can bring. Let's do it. Invite family and any friends you want. Your backyard is the perfect place for a party. What do you say?"

"We've had a few backyard office parties for Darlina's co-workers over the years and they always turned out great. I happen to know a few ol' pickers around here that would come and play in return for a chance to fill their bellies with fresh fish."

Hilda returned with several cold beers.

"And you damned well better play too." Claude paused to open the beer Hilda handed to him.

"That'd be a lot of fun. There's still some of Claude's family that I haven't met." Hilda said as she sat beside Claude.

Luke slapped his knee. "By God, we'll do it. Darlina can cook up some beans and I know the old boy that owns Catfish Corner in Abilene. We can pick up hushpuppies and coleslaw from him."

By the time Claude and Hilda left that evening, they'd made plans for a backyard party at Luke and Darlina's on the second weekend of October.

***

Luke went to work to salvage what he could of his old band equipment, and with a little help from a music store in Brown-wood, managed to piece together a small PA system.

As he refurbished what he'd used many years ago as his monitor speaker, he told Darlina of how no other bands were using monitors at that time. They'd called him crazy for having a speaker turned around facing the stage.

Nowadays, no band would consider getting on stage without them. Just another mark of how things had changed over the years and of how Luke had been a pioneer in his time.

Early on the morning of October 12th, he set up microphone stands leftover from the 60s on the rock patio along with the PA system.

Lily and Alexander had come in the night before for the party and to be of help. Sally drove from Louisiana and Judy joined in the party as well as Elora and a few of Darlina's co-workers.

Darlina and Lily bustled around like bees working a hive, decorating tables, opening umbrellas over them to provide shade while Hilda prepared the fish to be fried.

Claude lit a fire under his fish cooker. The weather turned out perfect and by noon succulent redfish sizzled in a vat of oil for the folks that drifted in. By the time the party got underway, close to forty people had gathered.

Luke flipped the switch on the PA system and stepped up to the mic. "We'd like to welcome everyone here today. There's plenty of fish, plenty of side dishes and we're gonna have plenty of music. So y'all sit back, relax and have a good time."

He watched as Darlina greeted each guest and thought about how she made everyone feel welcome. He knew this only added extra work to her already full days, but she appeared relaxed and happy. He could tell she was excited about the prospect of having music, and entertaining folks.

He marveled at how their love only increased with each day that passed. They knew each other's thoughts, fears and wishes. Hell, they even dreamed the same dream from time to time.

A case of nerves threatened to attack and Luke did his best to squelch them. What did he have to be nervous about? These were family and friends, and only a handful of people. And yet, the anticipation of holding his guitar and singing for them made his palms sweaty.

It had always been that way, though. He'd experienced that same feeling every time he got on stage, but in less than two minutes, they would vanish leaving him cool, collected and confident.

As soon as everyone had eaten their fill and settled back in lawn chairs, Luke invited some local musicians to kick off the entertainment.

After an hour passed, one of the musicians stepped up to the mic. "I think you've heard enough from us. How about we get Luke Stone up here to sing for you?"

Everyone applauded and cheered. Luke strode toward the makeshift stage with his guitar slung around his shoulders. He strummed a chord and began.

"I once had a sweetheart, the fairest of maidens
She outshined all others that I'd known by far
I had a friend named Big Harlan Taylor
Harlan had a rubber tired new shiny car
Oh the ways of the world and the wants of a woman
If I figured them all out, it would take many years…"

By the time he finished the song, the jittery nerves settled and he relaxed into an easy flow from one song to the next.

It wasn't a packed auditorium like he'd performed in many times during his life, but it was just as important and fulfilling to play for a handful of friends and family in his own backyard.

As twilight began to creep in, one-by-one, the guests took their leave. Not one person failed to thank Luke and Darlina and express what a wonderful afternoon it had been.

Once the last guest departed and tables had been cleared, they sat around a table drinking and talking.

"I think we ought to make this a yearly event, Luke. Everyone sure had a good time. Know what was the only thing missing?" Claude popped the top open on a cold beer.

"What was that Claude?"

"A damned fiddle. I sure do love the fiddle. Think maybe next year you can get a fiddle player to come?"

Luke chuckled. "I can probably do that." He turned to Darlina. "Honey, I think you oughta start singing some harmony with me. We have a whole year to practice."

"Oh Luke, I'd love that, but I never want to be an embarrassment to you."

"Bullshit! There is nothing you could do that would embarrass me." He strove to keep irritation out of his voice. Why did she always doubt herself? He turned to Lily. "And you, little lady, have a year to practice a song or two and get up there with us. You have a very special voice and this is a way it can be heard."

Lily smiled at her dad. "I'd really like that, Dad."

"Maybe I can sing some harmony with you." Darlina put her hand on her daughter's arm. Her laughter rang out. "We'll have a family band."

Claude roared and slapped the table. "Now that's what I'm talking about."

Luke looked around the table. He couldn't think of anything that would please him more than to have his family join him in making music. Funny, he'd never considered the possibility of that, and yet, why not?

He took a sip of Beam and Coke and leaned back looking up at the stars. "Look at all those twinkling stars up there. I like to think those are our loved ones who have passed on looking down on us smiling."

Claude joined in the stargazing. "You may be right, Luke. If they are, you know your mama and daddy are thrilled with what went on here today."

Luke cleared his throat. "They sure would have enjoyed this and Mom would've have joined right in with the singing and playing. I miss them."

Claude stood and stretched. "I'm beat. Let's call it a night. Thank you everyone, for all of your hard work today."

Luke stood and hugged his uncle. "You better get busy fishing. We're gonna need twice this much next year."

"I bet I can handle it. Come on, Hilda. Let's get going."

As farewells were exchanged, Luke reached for Darlina and brought her close. He loved the way her arm easily slid around his waist and how she leaned in slightly, just enough to speak volumes without saying a word.

He gave the stars one more glance and they made their way inside. It was a good day; a good beginning to something wonderful.

***

A few days later, Luke received a phone call from Josh Alan informing him that Texas Monthly had accepted the article.

He said Luke would be hearing from Joe Nick Potoski at the magazine headquarters in Austin within the next few weeks.

Luke thanked Josh Alan profusely and immediately called Darlina at work to share the news. He loved hearing the excitement in her voice. Somehow he knew this would be the catalyst for something else.

He'd learned in life that most things happened to set up the next scene. Thinking back, the events were a domino effect. First, Roxy and Judy Gordon coming into their lives, becoming such close friends, then Roxy's death, getting on stage and singing and then the interview. Who knew where it would go from here. Time would tell. But, everything seemed to be leading back to a second music career for Luke.

After several conversations with Joe Nick Potoski at Texas Monthly, he learned that the piece would appear in the January 2001 issue. They'd titled it *Outlaw Country*.

And what could be more appropriate for a man who called himself a rebel?

~Uncle Claude cooking fish~

Chapter 6

November 11, 2000, fell on a Saturday. Not only was it a national holiday, but it was the date Lily and Alexander had chosen to be married.

Glad she'd had time to train the new girl who worked for her in the Saturday Store, Darlina clarified final details. She'd been using high school girls since Nicole had left home to go to college, and it worked well.

But, this would be the first time she and Luke had both been away on a Saturday since opening the store. She couldn't help but feel apprehensive, even though Luke's nephew, Gary, promised to stay close by.

She'd loved going shopping with her two girls for wedding dresses and looking at tuxedos for the men back in the summer, and now the wedding was here.

Darlina and Luke arrived at the hotel in Dallas shortly after noon on Friday. Sally had asked to share their room and arrived later that afternoon along with the rest of family. After they'd settled, Darlina rang the rooms of her mother, aunt, sisters, Luke's son and wife, Martin and Stormi. They all gathered along with Lily, Alexander, Nicole and her boyfriend, Chris, for the wedding rehearsal at the church, a few blocks away in historic downtown Dallas. Darlina sat with her mother and aunt while watching the rehearsal and relished the giggles of her children.

Following the rehearsal, Lily and Alexander had made reservations for everyone at Spaghetti Warehouse in the heart of the giant city.

Unfamiliar with the streets, Darlina asked to follow someone to the restaurant. Nicole's boyfriend offered, but when a red light separated them, he didn't stop to wait for them.

Darlina struggled to remember the directions she'd been given, but they only got more and more lost. Luke's irritability grew with each passing moment.

A knot formed in her gut. She never wanted to upset Luke and even though it wasn't her fault, she knew he was growing more angry and upset by the minute.

After much difficulty, Darlina finally located the restaurant. Of course, they were late, but no one seemed to notice.

Everyone talked at once and a buzz of excitement filled the air. Before she knew it, Luke had consumed a large amount of alcohol. He refused to eat supper, stating he couldn't stomach Italian food, and as the alcohol took over, he became more vocal. Martin proceeded to join in with his father and the two of them became the life of the party.

After the dinner ended, she felt torn. She wanted to go with Sally and the girls back to the church to help decorate, but was afraid to leave Luke. What if he had another heart attack and she wasn't there to help him?

Great! How could he let himself get drunk at their daughter's wedding?

She knew he could feel her strained angry emotions but tried to paste on a smile and stay close by his side. With tears near the surface, they finally made it back to the hotel room. Tomorrow was an important day and red eyes wouldn't be good. Outraged, she couldn't stay quiet.

"Why, Luke? Why did you have to pull this tonight? It's Lily's wedding."

"Pull what? I was nice to everyone."

"But, honey, you're drunk."

He plopped down in a chair in the corner and closed his eyes. "So?"

Darlina sat on the side of the bed and tried to think of what to do. She spared a glance in his direction to find him staring back at her. He may as well have been a million miles away, with a great gaping abyss between them.

"Anything else you wanna say?" he growled.

"No," she whispered. "I guess not."

"What? I didn't hear you."

How could he turn like this? Where was the love? Her heart broke. "I said, no, I guess not."

He hiccupped and leaned back in the chair.

After several failed attempts, she gave up on convincing him to come to bed and crawled between the sheets. She buried her face in the pillow and sobbed silently, thankful that Sally had gone with the girls to the church.

If only she could understand what happened. Was it the emotion of Lily getting married that affected him so deeply? Was it being in the big city and so totally out of his element? Or maybe it was the struggle they had finding the restaurant. Questions rolled around with no answers. Her stomach churned and a lump the size of a boulder formed in her throat.

She heard his shoes hit the floor and hoped that maybe he was finally coming to bed. She rolled over to see Luke stretched out in the chair with his head back. At least he didn't leave the room because she knew that no matter how upset she was, she'd go find him.

When Sally tiptoed in later that night, Darlina sat up in the bed. Sally's eyes questioned and Darlina simply shrugged her shoulders and lay back down. She owed Sally a huge debt of gratitude for stepping up and helping Lily.

Sometime in the wee hours of morning, Darlina felt Luke slip into bed beside her. She breathed a sigh of relief and hoped they could sort through all of this once the wedding was over. But for now, everyone was in their places and the most important day of Lily's life would come front and center.

***

The next morning, with coffee in hand, Luke sat forlorn on the side of the bed. Darlina moved to sit beside him and rubbed his back. No matter how mad she was, the love was still there, but they would be having a conversation once the wedding was over.

When he looked over at her, his bloodshot eyes said more than any words could. She kissed his cheek and he closed his eyes. He didn't have to say he was sorry. His body language screamed it.

"Let's get some breakfast." Darlina stood and sat her coffee cup on the night stand beside the bed.

With one smooth motion, Luke pulled Darlina down on his lap and buried his face in her hair. They both looked up when Sally stirred and pushed her covers back.

"Good morning," Sally bounded out of bed. "Oh, wait until you see the church. It is absolutely beautiful and I had so much fun with the girls."

Darlina pushed herself up from Luke's lap. "Thank you for going, Sally. I can't wait to see it. Do you want any breakfast? We're about to head down."

"No, go ahead. I'm not much of a breakfast girl. I'll start ironing my dress and take a shower so you two can get ready when you get back."

Luke stood and sat his cup beside Darlina's. "We're having a wedding today, girls." He reached for Darlina's hand. "Let's go get some food."

***

By two o'clock that afternoon, all of the families gathered in the hotel lobby before going to the church. Eye drops had helped Darlina's appearance and she put on her happiest face.

She looked up in surprise when someone tapped her on the shoulder. Turning around, she came face-to-face with Will, her ex-husband and biological father of Lily and Nicole.

"Will. I didn't know you were coming." Sudden awkwardness so thick a knife couldn't cut it flew between them.

He stepped forward to embrace her. "I didn't want to miss my daughter's wedding."

Darlina's nose twitched. Damn! His body odor nearly knocked her down even though his shoulder-length blonde hair was wet and appeared to be freshly washed. Must be the clothes, she thought.

"It's good to see you." She stepped back.

Luke extended his hand. "Hey, man, glad you could make it." He put his arm around Darlina's shoulders.

Will nodded and moved away after shaking Luke's hand.

It was about time he stepped up and participated in something with his daughters, although she knew Lily would be embarrassed that he stank.

Once they reached the church, Luke went into the room with the groom and groomsmen while Darlina joined Lily, Nicole and the bridesmaids in a separate room.

Nicole ran to greet her mother. "Mom, can you help me with the zipper on this dress? It's not doing right."

"Of course, sweetie." She put her purse on a small table by the door. "Turn around and let me look at it."

Nicole turned around and Darlina saw that a piece of the fabric was caught in the zipper. She maneuvered it loose and zipped the dress. "You look absolutely radiant, Nicole."

She turned to Lily and her breath caught in her throat. "Oh honey, I'm so happy for you. You look like an angel straight from heaven." She embraced her daughter, taking care not to crush the delicate layers of lace and satin. "You're the most stunning bride I've ever seen."

Lily returned her mother's hug. "I'm happy too, Mom. And everything's going so smooth. I thought weddings were supposed to be chaotic."

"Oh, sweetheart, you have no idea."

"Why? What happened besides Dad and Martin having too much to drink last night?" Lily giggled and turned to reach for her earrings.

"That pretty much covers it. Do I look okay?"

"Mom you're always beautiful, but I don't remember ever seeing you in a hat." Lily giggled again. "It looks cute though. Here are your flowers." Lily handed Darlina a floral box.

Darlina opened the box to find yellow and white lilies with tiny burgundy rosebuds nestled amongst them on a wristband. She buried her nose in the bouquet and inhaled the sweet fragrance. How perfectly they matched Lily's spirit. She snapped the band to her left wrist. "These are amazing, Lily. You did a great job putting all of this together, honey."

Darlina adjusted her hat, wishing she'd worn something more fitting to this magnificent event.

Lily picked up a white satin-clad box. "Can you fasten my necklace for me, Mom?"

"Of course." Darlina's eyes misted when she saw the gleaming pearls inside. "This is your day, sweetie, and the most important thing is that you're one hundred percent sure about marrying Alexander."

"Yep, I'm very sure. Did you see Will this morning?"

"Yes. Did you?"

"No, but Nicole did. I'm sure I'll see him at the reception."

Nicole spoke up. "I saw him earlier. He didn't recognize me at first. I'm actually surprised he's here."

Darlina didn't mention the body odor. It was best left unsaid. She was determined to make this day perfect for Lily. She dropped the subject and focused on the last minute details.

As time for the ceremony grew closer, Darlina turned toward the door. "I'm going to go check on Dad before I take my place in the chapel. I'm so proud of you girls and the women you've grown into. I love you."

"Love you too, Mom." Both girls hugged her once more.

Darlina thought about the happy energy of her daughters while she walked toward the room where she would find Luke. They were so vibrant, so full of life and hopes and dreams.

She knocked on the closed door. Alexander opened it a crack. "Everything going okay in here?"

"Other than me being so nervous I can hardly stand it?"

Darlina laughed. "Yes, other than that."

Luke popped his head around the door. "Hi, beautiful."

"Hi yourself. I just wanted to check on you before I went into the chapel." She refused to let a smile form at his boyish action. She had to stay mad for a while longer.

"We're all good. Sally pinned our boutonnieres on a little bit ago. I'm just trying to keep these boys entertained."

"I bet you are," she said wryly. "I'll see you inside."

Luke threw her a kiss and she turned on her heel. How could he pretend that nothing was wrong? Men!

She wasn't going to let it go that easy.

The usher stood at the entry to the chapel, ready to escort her to her seat. Darlina looked over the gathering crowd.

She noticed that Will sat alone a few rows back from the family pews. Some part of her felt a little sorry for him, but she quickly reminded herself that he was the one who'd chosen to isolate himself from his children. When he looked at her, she thought she saw a complete lack of emotion. Did he feel nothing?

She joined her mother and aunt who'd already been seated.

The stained glass windows of the church perfectly accented the day lilies in varying brilliant colors. Tears stung the back of her eyes at her daughter's gift for selecting things that filled the spirit as well as the visual. She took in the hundred or so tea candles placed around the altar that gave the chapel an ethereal glow.

The crowning touch was a unity candle sitting on a stand waiting to be lit.

Gentle flowing music from the organist began and the bridesmaids entered with their escorts. Then the best man and Nicole entered the chapel. She walked slowly down the aisle and took her place on the left side of the podium, confident and smiling. When had she gotten so grown up?

Alexander entered next and stood beside his best man. Darlina could almost see his knees shaking and smiled inwardly. That he had a case of nerves said a lot. There was no doubt he cared deeply for Lily.

Everyone stood with the first notes of the wedding march. Her tears fell unchecked when Luke came into view with Lily on his arm.

No princess ever born could have been more breathtaking than Lily that day. Her face glowed and her eyes twinkled. Her white satin gown billowed around her and her strawberry blonde hair piled high on her head held the exquisite lace veil in place.

Darlina's heart nearly burst with love for them. Luke smiled at her as they passed and his eyes said, "Everything is going to be all right."

Once Luke handed Lily over to Alexander, he joined Darlina and took her hand. His fingers wrapped easily around hers as love washed over her. It was all she could do to hold back sobs.

Twice she saw Luke reach for his handkerchief and wipe his eyes. Then she knew. The emotions he felt had overwhelmed him and he'd let the alcohol sneak up on him. She could feel that he was sorry without him ever speaking a word.

However, she also knew once the wedding and reception were over and they were on their way home, she'd make it very clear to Luke Stone that never again would she tolerate him losing control to liquor again.

With squared shoulders she listened to each word in the vows her daughter exchanged with her new husband.

She hoped they could weather the storms that would inevitably come their way, and that they'd never forget the promises they were making to each other.

Marriages were full of trials and hard times as well as happy and good times. There was no denying that she loved the man sitting beside her on the polished church pew.

There was no denying that they'd come a long way and no denying that they weren't finished yet. Not now, not ever.

Her attention was drawn back to the couple as the minister pronounced them man and wife and they sealed it with a nervous kiss.

As soon as the ceremony ended, Lily and Alexander joined arms and strolled back down the aisle with smiles as big as Texas. The rest of the wedding party filed out behind them and the guests gathered in the reception hall to wait for the new couple.

Once they'd finished participating in the photographs, Luke and Darlina joined Darlina's mother, aunt and sister at a round table in the reception hall.

Will hesitantly approached them. "Do you guys mind if I sit with you?"

Luke motioned to an empty chair. "Of course not. Have a seat."

Will leaned toward Darlina. "Lily and Nicole sure are beautiful young women."

Darlina nodded. Conversation with Will about daughters he'd basically abandoned did not interest her. She quickly turned and began talking to her sister.

She could hear Luke making polite conversation with Will and was thankful for his intervention.

Soon the bride and groom made their appearance. When they walked through the door, everyone stood and applauded. Lily and Alexander made their way around the room, greeting each of their guests. If it was possible, Lily radiated even more than she did before the ceremony.

Soon, she and Alexander stood behind the table that held the elegant three-tiered wedding cake with the same brilliant day lilies adorning it. The best man stood to make the traditional toast.

Once he sat down, Nicole took the microphone and spoke about the closeness she and her sister had shared through the years, and then managed to dredge up some embarrassing stories which had everyone laughing, including Lily.

Darlina froze when Will stood and walked toward the front. What was he up to now?

He reached for the microphone and faced the crowd. "I just want to say how happy I am to have been here today. And I want to thank Luke and Darlina for doing such a good job raising my daughters." He turned toward Lily and Alexander. "I wish you many happy years and may you come to know the Great I Am." With that, he laid the microphone on a table and exited the room.

A moment of awkward silence followed. Darlina breathed a sigh. At least he'd kept it short. She felt sure no one in the room knew what he meant by the Great I Am, or that it had to do with his latest cult following.

Lily reached for the knife to cut the cake. Urges came from the guests to smear it on Alexander's face, but from her sweet smile, it was obvious they'd agreed not to do that to each other.

Bottles of champagne made their way around the room and everyone joined in the celebration with the party lasting into the evening. At dusk, a white horse-drawn carriage arrived to take Alexander and Lily on a ride around the historic square and to their hotel room.

Everyone who remained at the reception moved outside to see the bride and groom off. Just when Darlina thought every emotion in her had been spent, the sight of Lily in her wedding dress sitting like Cinderella in the carriage took her breath.

Once the carriage pulled away, Sally turned to Darlina. "Why don't ya'll go on back to the hotel and I'll stay to help clean up. I need to keep busy so I won't think about Jim and how much I'm missing him right now."

Darlina hugged her friend. "Thank you, Sally. I love you." Then she whispered in Sally's ear. "I hate to tell you, but Jim is here with us. We just can't see him."

Sally smiled and blinked away emotion.

Luke and Darlina said their goodbyes to family, then gathered their things and made their way back to the hotel, exhausted.

With wedding clothes carefully hung and lights out, Darlina and Luke slid under the covers.

Luke opened his mouth once to speak but she put her fingers on his lips. "Not tonight, sweetheart. We can talk tomorrow."

He kissed her fingers and tucked the covers around her.

Tomorrow was a new day. A new beginning in many ways...A new beginning for Lily and Alexander and perhaps even a new beginning for Luke and Darlina.

~Lily and Alexander after wedding ceremony~

Chapter 7

The next day, as Darlina drove home from Dallas, she and Luke talked.

"Baby, I'm sorry. I don't know how many ways I can say it. You've gotta believe that I never intended to get drunk. Things just got away from me." Luke reached for her hand, only to have her pull away and place it on the steering wheel.

With tears on her cheeks, Darlina replied, "I know you didn't, Luke, but the truth is that you did and you acted an ass to me. I don't understand how you could shut me out like that."

Luke sighed. "You knew when you married me that I'm not perfect. I screwed up. I think what really got me wound up was the panic of being lost trying to get to the restaurant and there wasn't a damn thing I could do to help you find it."

"I know. But, for you to get mad at me because I couldn't find it wasn't right. It was our daughter's wedding. We were both wearing our emotions on our sleeves. Those are only excuses."

Luke sighed. "I wasn't mad at you for getting lost. I was mad that Nicole's boyfriend didn't wait for us. I just took it out on you. I know that, and I'm truly sorry."

"I'm sorry too. Here's one thing you have to know. Life is too short and I don't ever want us to go through anything like that again."

"You have my word."

"I'm serious, Luke."

"So am I. Please forgive me."

"I can forgive, but I can't forget yet."

Silence fell around them.

Even though Darlina's insides settled, she knew it would take time to heal the wound that Luke's actions had caused. It couldn't be cured with just a few words.

She also knew in her heart she'd already forgiven him. She simply couldn't let him know yet.

The miles clicked off and by the time they made it home, they were physically and emotionally drained.

Nothing in life was worth discord between them.

Darlina knew that Luke never claimed to be perfect or really even more than common. But to her, he was anything but common. He had drive and such amazing artistic talent. And he had proven that as long as he drew a breath, he'd never stop working, dreaming or building for them.

If determination was any measure of success, then Luke Stone was as successful as any man could be.

But, it would be a while before she could totally forget what had happened in Dallas. And she'd make damned sure he remembered. They had some mending to do.

***

The following Monday morning, Darlina sat across the desk from her friend Elora. When she finished relating the details of the wedding, Elora reached for her coffee cup.

"Sounds to me like Luke had more emotion than he could contain. And, you know how he sometimes freaks out in crowds anyway."

Darlina sighed. "I know. But, all I could think about was not letting it ruin Lily's big day."

"I'm sure you did your best and from what you said, Lily was oblivious to it all, so that was good."

"I suppose you are right, but I'm still mad at Luke."

Elora grinned. "I'm sure he'll find away to make it up to you."

Darlina stood. "We've got to get to work. Thanks for listening, Elora."

"Anytime." Elora flipped the switch to her computer.

Later that morning, Darlina sat her desk working when the door chimed and a local florist entered with a large bouquet of roses.

Darlina got up and approached the counter. "Who is the lucky lady today?"

The young man turned over the card pinned to the bow and read, "Darlina Stone."

Darlina gasped. "Oh, that's me."

"Well then congratulations." The young man handed the vase full of aromatic red roses to her.

She took the vase, thanked him and sat them on the corner of her desk. As she buried her nose in the sweet flowers, tears filled her eyes. "Oh, Luke, how can I stay mad at you?" she thought and reached for the phone.

***

On a mid-December day, Luke opened the mailbox to find a complimentary copy of Texas Monthly. He hurried into the house and tore open the envelope. After reaching for his reading glasses, he scanned the index then turned to page seventy-four.

With hands trembling slightly, he held the publication and let reality soak in. *Outlaw Country* was emblazoned across the top of the page. Beneath it read, *'Luke Stone was a rising star of Texas music — until he and one of his bandmates went to prison for bank robbery.'*

He chuckled out loud at the picture of him along with his band standing on a railroad track, dressed like banditos and brandishing pistols. He knew Josh Alan had found it ironic that the prosecutor had used this picture in the bank robbery trials as evidence. What he didn't know was Josh had chosen it for the magazine piece.

He read through to the end and slowly removed his glasses. It was good, and even fairly accurate. He took a deep breath and let the feeling in his chest expand to full-blown gratitude. He hadn't sought this publicity. It had come to him out of the blue and here it was in print. Not only just in print, but in a magazine with a large distribution.

Glancing at the clock, he realized that Darlina would be off from work in ten minutes.

He picked up the phone and dialed.

"Thank you for calling the Department of Human Services. How may I help you?" her cheerful voice answered.

"Honey, it's me. Can you run by Shoppin' Basket on your way home today and see if they have any of the Texas Monthly magazines on the shelf yet?"

"Of course. Anything else I need to pick up while I'm there?"

"Nope, just hurry your sweet little ass home."

"Okay, baby. I'll be there in a few minutes." Her laugh tinkled through the phone line.

"I've got something here you'll want to see."

He knew her curiosity would be piqued.

In less than fifteen minutes, she burst through the door.

"They didn't have any magazines yet. Dennis said they'll get a delivery tomorrow. What do you have to show me?" She shucked her coat and gloves and tossed them aside.

"Come over here." Luke patted the arm of his chair.

She sat and draped her arm across Luke's shoulders. "Okay, I'm ready. What is it?"

The magazine lay on the end table next to his chair and he reached for it. "This came in the mail today."

She gasped. "Oh how wonderful! I can't wait to read it."

"There's a couple of things that ain't exactly accurate, but overall it's pretty damn good." He handed the magazine to Darlina.

She stood and moved to her chair. He sipped his tea while she read.

When she looked up, he saw tears glistening. "Oh baby, this is excellent. I love the way he described our place here as a compound. I hadn't thought of it like that and the detail he gave to Daralu Records was very visual. Even if I'd never seen it, I think I'd get the idea. I remember him laughing when you told him how we'd come up with the company name by putting our two names together."

"Yeah, and I didn't know he'd use the part about the kid asking me how to rob a bank, but it was a great way to start out."

"It's amazing. I'm absolutely proud of you." She laid the magazine back on the end table and returned to his chair.

She wrapped her arms around his neck and slid onto his lap.

"Honey, I'm just an ol' convict guitar picker, but you, you're my shining star. You're the reason for everything I do and I tell everyone what an angel you are." He lowered his head to meet her warm kiss.

The glow in her eyes when she looked up told him all he ever needed or wanted to know. With a deep sigh, he silently offered up a prayer of thanks. The Great Spirit had smiled warmly upon him once again.

Then he extracted her arms from around his neck and gave her a gentle push. "While you get us a bite to eat, I'll cut this out and make a mockup. Maybe you could sneak making a few copies of it at work tomorrow."

She grinned. "I'm sure I can manage that. Supper will be ready in half an hour."

While pots and pans rattled, he sat at the kitchen table with scissors, blank paper and glue and arranged the columns of the article so that they could easily be copied.

"Who knows where any of this will go. I've always believed that the harder I work, the luckier I get."

Darlina turned from the stove. "Baby, if work has anything to do with luck, we both ought to be the luckiest two people alive."

Luke stood and in two strides, had her in his arms. "We are."

***

Christmas came and went quietly for Luke and Darlina that year. With Nicole in Colorado and unable to come home and Lily and Alexander celebrating Christmas in their new home, they quietly passed the holiday alone.

Both he and Darlina agreed they would have their children with them next Christmas when it rolled around again.

Judy brought news that Christmas, that she was leaving Coleman County and moving to Dallas. Both Luke and Darlina thought this would be good for her. At least she could get the proper medical care she required to keep her seizures under control. It also helped that her oldest son who already lived in Dallas, had married a nurse. With some sadness, they said their goodbyes.

***

As an early spring began to chase the cold winter days away and tiny green buds dotted the bare tree limbs, Luke sought opportunities to play music. He started booking shows locally and had no trouble gathering musicians who were happy to accompany him.

Before long, he was playing several times a month and getting calls almost daily from someone wanting him to perform. He'd convinced Darlina to sing backup harmony with him on a few standards, and that added an even deeper satisfaction and meaning to all of it. With her at his side, there was nothing he couldn't do. It felt good to be getting back in the game again.

On a particularly warm day, Luke put the finishing touches on an instrument he'd always dreamed of building. He liked the sound of the banjo, but had never learned to play, so when he had the chance to buy one at a cheap price, he'd decided then and there to put a guitar neck on it. It would be a combination of a guitar and banjo.

What would he call it? Maybe a Bantar? Or perhaps a Gitjo. He liked the sound of that.

He looked up when Darlina waltzed through the door of the shop. "Hi, sugar. Look at this." He held it up.

She joined Luke, tiptoeing to place a kiss on his cheek. "What is it?"

"I don't know. I think I'll call it a Gitjo. The other day, on ol' boy sold me this banjo and I decided to put a guitar neck on it so I could play it."

Darlina reached for the instrument and plucked the strings. "This is pretty cool. Luke, do you think I'm too old to learn to play guitar?"

"Hell, no. If you want to learn to play, I'll give you this Gitjo. I'm not quite finished with it yet, but when I am, you can have it."

His heart turned flip-flops at the shine in her eyes when she looked up. "I really would like to learn. It'd be fun to play along with you, and maybe even write songs together."

"Then by god, I'll teach you. I drew up chord charts while I was in prison and I can show you finger positions, but more than anything it is lots and lots of practice."

"Oh thank you, baby. I will learn quick."

"Now don't go gettin' stars in your eyes. It's hard work learning to play an instrument. Your fingers will get sore and maybe even crack and bleed before you get calluses built up, but if you stick with it, you can learn."

"You'll see. I'll work hard. I've loved singing with you, and I'm starting to get over a little of my stage fright. Still, playing an instrument would be awesome. When I first met you, I was very careful not to let you know how I'd always dreamed of singing on stage or you'd have had me up there with you."

Luke took the instrument from Darlina and gathered her close. "Sweetheart, anything you want to do, I'll move heaven and earth to try and make it happen."

"I know and I love you for that. I really do want to learn to play an instrument and I think this Gitjo is just what I need to get started."

"Then consider it yours. I'll have it finished up in a day or two and you can plunk on it all you want to."

Luke meant his words. Any desire Darlina had, he wanted to make it come true for her. He knew she did the same for him, and as he so often did, he wondered how he'd ever gotten so lucky.

***

The next trip to Abilene for an appointment with Dr. Robertson brought encouraging news to Luke and Darlina.

They both listened intently as Dr. Robertson described a new therapeutic treatment.

"It's Hyperbaric Chamber therapy," the doctor explained. "You are enclosed in a plexi-glass tube and pure oxygen is pumped into it at two and a half times greater than the normal pressure in the atmosphere. We've already seen great results in increased blood flow to restricted areas. Even though we've been able to open some of the blocked arteries with surgery, they're only going to plug again with the plaque that builds up. I think you might benefit from this oxygen therapy and I'd like to refer you for treatment."

"Where is it, and how many times a week would I have to do it?" Luke had dared to hope that the last surgery resolved the circulation problem, but Dr. Robertson had explained it was the nature of the disease.

"Next door in the hospital. I'd let Dr. Buman make the call on how often you'd need to do the treatment, but I truly feel it might help. Otherwise we're looking at another bilateral bypass sometime in the near future. I'm not saying it's a cure, but it definitely can't hurt."

Darlina looked up from her notepad. "Then I say we try it. What do you have to lose, Luke?"

"I reckon you're right. The circulation in my legs is getting worse again and even though things got better sexually after the surgery, I'm struggling again. If it'll help, then I say we go for it."

"I'll call Dr. Buman and you'll hear from his office about an appointment."

"Hey, Doc, how about a hot tub? Do you think that would make any difference?"

"Of course it would. Anything that increases the blood flow is beneficial."

"I don't suppose there's a prescription you can write for it so that maybe insurance would cover it?"

"I can write a prescription but all it'll do is let you purchase one without having to pay any sales tax."

"That's better than nothing. Go ahead and write the script."

Once they left the doctor's office, Luke drove straight to Lowe's. After looking at the hot tubs on display and talking with a salesman, they purchased one and made arrangements for delivery in two weeks.

Back in the car, Luke laid out the work he'd need to do in order to prepare for it. "I wanna put it in the bunkhouse. I'll take the bed out and set the spa inside. That way, we can use it year-round."

"That's a great idea, honey. I know this is for therapeutic purposes, but I'm really excited. I feel rich and spoiled." She laughed.

"Sugar, if there is one thing I want in life, it's to spoil you. I think I'll put river rock gravel down under the floor and use treated lumber so any drainage won't rot the boards. I've got a shit load of work to do in less than two weeks."

"Yes, but you always have work to do, honey. It never ends."

Luke chuckled. "And it won't until I draw my last breath. I want to stop at Hank's music store and pick up a few things before we head home."

"Okay. The two guys that own Hank's are really nice and they love hearing your stories. I think you've become some sort of a hero to them."

"Lord, they're scraping the bottom of the barrel there. But, I do like shootin' the shit with them. I remember when that music store belonged to a good friend of mine. I bought lots of instruments, strings and picks there, back in the day."

Darlina laid her hand on Luke's knee. "Honey, if I haven't told you lately, I couldn't be happier that you're turning back to music. It completes you."

"Full circle, as they say." Luke chuckled. "Who knows? Maybe I'll get another real shot at the game before I check out. Only this time, it'll be a whole different set of rules."

~Luke and Darlina performing at a benefit in Mason, Texas~

~Darlina holding the Gitjo that Luke created~

~Luke holding the Gitjo~

Chapter 8

Exactly two weeks later, Lowe's delivered and installed the hot tub in the bunkhouse where Luke had finished preparations.

Luke began driving back and forth to Abilene three times a week for the new innovative Hyperbaric therapy.

He couldn't have been more proud of the way Darlina took to learning to play the Gitjo, even making time to practice before she went to work each morning. She'd gotten pretty darn good on it in a short period of time, and Luke decided her next birthday present would be a new guitar. Her birthday was months away, and the many trips to Abilene gave him the opportunity to find the perfect one for her.

***

Even though it was nearing the end of spring, the air held an unseasonal chill and rain drizzled from the gray sky. As far as

Luke Stone was concerned, July couldn't come soon enough to suit him. The more blood thinners they put him on, the colder he stayed.

He shivered and turned up the heat in the sign shop, then reached for his brushes. Before he could get the paint can opened he heard a car stop in the drive.

He stepped through the door closing it behind him in time to see Mark and Jerry from Hank's Music Store in Abilene, climbing out of Mark's pickup.

"Hey, man," Jerry called.

Luke pulled his rain jacket tighter around his shoulders, strode toward them and shook hands. "What are you guys doing down here in Povertyville?"

"We came to see you." Mark grinned. "Did we catch you at a bad time?"

"Nah. Just working on a sign for the liquor store down the street. Let's get out of this rain. What can I do for you fellas?"

The men followed Luke into the sign shop. "Mark and I have something we want to discuss with you."

"Let me lock up here and we'll go next door to the music room."

"Cool," Jerry said.

In two short minutes, they walked next door to the building that housed the collection of vinyl records, and Luke's music memorabilia museum. He put the key in the lock and pushed the door open.

After they'd settled and Luke cranked up an electric heater, he sat down and faced them. "Okay. I'm all ears."

"Well, we've been thinking." Mark glanced at Jerry. "We're sorta fans of yours and we love the music history you represent."

"Yeah?" Luke leaned back in his chair.

"I know you're probably gonna say no, but at least promise you'll listen to what we have to say," Jerry added.

"I'm known to be a fair man most of the time. I'll listen." By now Luke was beginning to wonder what the two had up their sleeves, but he'd hear them out. "Can I get y'all something to drink?"

"No, thanks. We're okay. Did you know we have a recording studio in the back of Hank's?"

"Don't guess I had any reason to know that. What's it got to do with me?"

"We'd like to put out a CD of your music." Mark softened his voice. "We feel drawn to do this, Luke. Not that you're fixing to die or anything, but to give you another shot at getting some of your never-heard music out there."

"Hell, man, I'd love that, but I can tell you right now that I don't have the money for a project like that."

"Well, that's just it." Jerry leaned forward. "Mark and I would record and produce the CD at no cost to you. The only thing you'd have to do is pay the musicians."

Luke stared, fighting back emotion so thick it threatened to strangle him. "You'd do that for me?" He cleared his throat, deeply touched by their generosity.

"Yes sir, we've talked a lot about it and feel strongly that we need to do this."

"I don't know. It'd mean lots of trips to Abilene. I'm having some health problems and don't know for sure that I could hold up to it. I'll need to talk it over with Darlina."

"We understand that. And we're not in a hurry. This is our slow time of the year and don't have anything booked in the studio. You'd be doing us a favor." Mark shifted in his chair. "And we'd like to be known as the ones who put out your return album."

Jerry added, "You could record anything you want, new or old. Do you have anything we could listen to?"

"Sure. I've taken a lot of stuff off the old reel-to-reel tapes and put on cassettes from the prison recordings. And, I've got lots of really old stuff from the sixties." He removed the cover from his player system and rummaged through his tape box. "You sure you want to hear this shit?" This could be a dream come true. A chance to release some of his songs using modern equipment and professional musicians couldn't be lightly dismissed.

The two nodded and settled back in their chairs.

For the next two hours, Luke played song after song, pausing to tell a story or two in between.

He glanced up when he heard a car door, surprised to see it had turned dark outside.

He stepped to the door and waved to Darlina. "Over here, honey. We've got company." He held the door until she dashed inside, holding her jacket over her head.

Mark and Jerry stood.

"Oh hi, guys. What in the world are you doing in Coleman?"

Jerry gave her a brief hug. "We came to see Luke. He can tell you all about it. We've lost track of the time and are going to have to run."

"Yeah, my wife will be wondering where I am." Mark hugged Darlina. "Guess you got here just in time to tell us bye." He turned to Luke. "Think about what we said and let us know what you decide. We're dead serious about this."

Luke nodded. "I really appreciate your confidence in me. I'll get back with you in a few days."

As soon as he closed the door behind them, he turned to Darlina. "Sweetheart, you're not going to believe this."

She stood quietly and listened while Luke told her everything, then reached for his hand. "Honey, I don't see that there's a decision to make. This is a chance to put out a CD for very little money. I'm actually blown away by the offer."

"I don't want to jump at it. I need to see if it feels right. It'd mean a lot of late nights and trips to Abilene after work." Luke slid his arm around her waist realizing they hadn't taken time to sit.

"I'm up for that. It would be exciting."

"It's not all glamour, sugar. It's a lot of hard work. We'd first have to choose what songs to record, then work on arrangements and musicians. I need to make a run over to Brownwood tomorrow and see if Bill Graham is around anywhere. He's the best bass player on the planet and I hear that he plays a mean fiddle and mandolin too."

Luke sensed excitement bubbling inside Darlina and saw the reflection of it in her clear blue eyes. He didn't want to squash that, but did want her to realize what undertaking a project of this size would involve.

He also knew that this opportunity could possibly open a whole new career for him. If nothing more, it would provide a professional demo of songs to pitch to the big heads.

Brushing a stray hair from Darlina's face, he said, "I'm going to call my old friend, Tommy Overstreet, in the morning and talk this over with him. He has more experience in the music business than anyone else I know."

"That's a great idea. I already have some songs in mind that I think would be great, but we can save all of those details for later after you've decided to do it." She reached up and put her hand behind his neck. "I love you, baby, and I'll be thrilled if you decide to record."

He leaned down and kissed her, then patted her bottom. "I know you will, darlin'. I just don't want to put even more burdens on you. Let's go to the house."

Darlina gathered her purse and waited under the porch awning while Luke locked the door.

Luke gazed up at the dark clouds rumbling across the Texas sky and gave a silent prayer of thanks once again to the Great Spirit.

They dashed to the door of the trailer and Luke held it open for her.

"Why don't you make something easy for supper tonight, sweetheart?"

"Okay." Darlina lay her purse on the table and kicked off her shoes.

Luke strode to his guitar case, opened it and slung the guitar strap over his shoulders. He tuned it and strummed while Darlina rattled pots and pans in the kitchen.

He turned over in his mind what Mark and Jerry proposed. This was an opportunity not to be taken lightly. A list of songs ran through his head.

He thought of all the hours he'd spent in prison putting together a makeshift studio out of broken pieces of electronics so he'd have a way to record the songs he was writing behind bars.

The warden had been hesitant in giving him permission to build it, and made it clear they'd provide no funding for the project. It came together with pure dedication, will and perseverance. And even though it wasn't a state-of-the-art studio, he'd managed to record many songs before leaving.

And now, a new chance with modern technology presented itself. It would be a far cry from Leavenworth prison, for sure.

By the time Darlina put plates on the table, he had the beginning of a new song. He felt energized. "Listen to this before we eat, darlin'."

Darlina perched on the edge of the chair. "I've been listening and I like the chord progression. Sing what you've got."

He strummed an E chord.

"Remember when I said it more often, how much I love you?
That I knew there would never be another
I'd want no one but you?
Well, honey, I still do…"

He looked up to see tears clinging to Darlina's eyelashes. "That's beautiful, Luke."

He put the guitar on the stand and gathered her in his arms. "Sweetheart, I don't ever mean to make you cry." He brushed a stray tear from her cheek with his rough thumb.

"You're not making me cry because I'm sad. It's just that I feel so much love for you and sometimes it spills out my eyes."

"Hell, baby, that's another song. I've gotta write that line down before I forget it." He gave her a playful shove and grinned.

She sniffled and laughed. "That's right. Go ahead and steal my lines."

"Everything I write. Everything I own, is all yours. When I'm gone, I hope that I've managed to leave something worth a damn for you."

"Honey, just look around. You've graced our home with the most beautiful artwork, both ceramics and paintings, not to mention the leather and bead work. You're leaving me plenty, but I don't want to talk about that. You aren't going anywhere for a long time. You've got a CD to make."

Luke ran his fingers through his hair and stood. "We'll see about that. Right now, I'm ready for some vittles."

They sat at the small table and shared a simple meal. As soon as his plate was empty, Luke headed back to the living room and a writing tablet.

After a few minutes, he called to Darlina. "Honey, come in here. I want to read this to you."

She took a seat beside him. "Okay. I'm listening."

He cleared his throat.

"If the end of the world should come tomorrow
Or whatever may come my way
There'll be no sorrow because I loved you today
Should the sun refuse to shine anymore
Blue skies turn to gray
I'll be happy as before because I loved you today."

"Oh sweetheart, I love you so much." Darlina moved toward him.

"I mean every word of it, darlin'." He captured her soft moist lips and murmured, "I truly mean every word."

Chapter 9

Three weeks later, after spending full day in San Angelo exploring the many thrift stores in search of treasures for the Saturday Store, Luke and Darlina headed home.

Their conversation soon turned to Mark and Jerry's proposal and the CD.

"I truly don't know why you're hesitating, Luke." Darlina nestled her hand in his free one.

"I just need a sign. Something to show me it's right. You know how I am. In spite of all they're offering, it'll still involve a huge commitment of time and money." He glanced over at her. Even with mussed hair from the Texas wind, she was beautiful to him. Somehow he never seemed able make her truly understand that.

"A chance like this might not come along again. I'd hate to see you miss it." She reached into her purse for a brush.

"I don't wanna miss it either. It's that damned ol' Indian medicine. I need a sign. I don't expect you to understand."

"And yet I do." She sighed and gazed out the window at the deepening evening shadows. "I'm really worried about you, honey. Even after the hyperbaric treatments, you're still having problems. I could tell it hurt you to walk today."

"Yeah well, don't forget I'm a tough ol' bird." Luke chuckled. "My left leg is throbbin' like a sick Robin's ass right this minute, but we've got a hot tub waitin' at home to crawl into."

"The hot tub was one of the best investments we've ever made…that and the dishwasher."

Luke suddenly braked. "Did you see that?"

"What?" She peered out the window through the deepening shadows.

"I don't know, but I have to turn around and go back."

"What do you think you saw?"

"An owl perched on a broken fence post beside the road. They don't naturally roost like that or at least I've never seen one. You know how I am about owls. They're my messengers." After checking both ways, he whirled the car around.

As he drove slowly along the shoulder, the headlights picked up the silhouette ahead. He switched off the radio and slowed to a crawl.

"I'll be damned. Look at that magnificent bird, just sitting there. It's definitely an owl and the hairs on the back of my neck are standing on end."

"It's beautiful," Darlina whispered.

Just then the owl took flight, heading directly for the vehicle, and then swooped up and over the top.

Silence filled the car.

Luke's voice was hushed when he finally spoke. "There was my sign." He turned toward Darlina. "This is what I was waiting on. I'll do the CD. That was my message."

"Oh Luke, it'll be wonderful." She leaned across the seat and kissed him. "Together we can do this."

Luke put the car in gear and turned around again. Thoughts spun out of control. Bits and pieces of songs jumped in and out. Which ones to use? Which ones to cull?

He remembered his conversation with his old friend, Tommy Overstreet, and the support and encouragement he'd shown. Yes, the signs were all there now. He'd call Mark and Jerry tomorrow and start putting this together.

He silently thanked his owl friend and the Great Spirit.

Luke's tone grew somber. "I want you to remember something, sweetheart. When I pass from this life, you're going to hear two sounds; a train whistle and the hooting of an owl."

Darlina turned to face him. "You've told me that before and I won't forget, but you aren't going anywhere for a long time, remember?" She fidgeted with her hands in her lap. "Baby, how do you know what your spirit animal is?"

Luke stared straight ahead. "It's a gradual process really. You see them often and start to take notice. You can even dream of them. We all have animals that are a part of us, part of our journey."

"I've been seeing lots of hawks lately. Do you think that could be one of my animal totems?"

"Sure. Only you know. I've been aware of owls since I was a little boy. I would see them at the oddest times and places, just like today. Then when I was in prison and studied American Indian beliefs, I realized how powerful that was and understood. Ever since then, they've been my guide. That is why I say you will hear them when I leave this body."

Darlina was silent for a few miles. "When I practiced meditation and studied Eastern religion, I started to see how similar all of the beliefs are. The American Indians and Eastern Indians had a lot of things in common. Funny, that each of us wound up studying a different one of them."

"I learned much about life and nature from the American Indian teachings. That's why I do smoke ceremony and give thanks to the Great Spirit."

Darlina reached for his hand. "I often think that if life hadn't pulled us apart when it did and sent us in such different directions, we wouldn't be the people we are today. We each needed to learn some life lessons before we could ever be together."

He squeezed her hand. "Yep, I totally agree, but I damned sure didn't think I needed to stay locked up for so long. I think I had learned what I needed to in the first five years. The other ten was just spent trying to be patient."

"I love you, Luke," she whispered.

He grinned. "I heard that, sweetheart and I double it."

***

With typical Luke Stone focus and concentrated energy, a list of songs soon formed. He had some favorites and some he believed in, but also had wisdom enough to know his view might be out-of-date or old-fashioned.

So, he listened carefully to what Mark and Jerry had to say, constantly asked Darlina for her opinion, and then mailed CDs to a handful of people to collect votes on favorite songs.

He even gathered a few songs written by his friends, Tommy Overstreet and Bill Graham, for consideration to include on the album.

So far, none stood out as a title track.

***

During the long years of incarceration, Luke had spent endless hours writing poetry and doing intricate pen and ink drawings. He called the compilation of poems and art *Etchings in Stone*.

It seemed a fitting title for the CD and he already had the artwork to go with it, taken from the cover of the poetry book. Now, all he needed was a song with the same title.

Sonny Throckmorton, renowned Nashville songwriter, had moved to Brownwood recently and Luke met him through his old friend, Bill Graham. So, Luke asked Sonny to think about writing the song with him and he promised that he'd get around to it.

Luke and Darlina tossed around possible lines, but nothing felt right.

Finally, the song came from an unexpected source.

Luke listened intently while John Beam, the young man from Mason whom Luke had mentored thirty years ago, sang what he'd been inspired to write. Even through the phone lines, Luke could feel the strength and conviction of the song. Tears threatened to choke Luke and once again the hair on the back of his neck stood up. Confirmation. John had written the perfect lyrics to *Etchings in Stone*.

"There once lived a man who did etchings in stone. He told other's stories but could not tell his own. He labored away 'til he'd get it right. Seemed he'd take forever 'cause that stone told their life..."

Luke couldn't wait for Darlina to get home that day, and as soon as she walked through the door, he asked her to pick up the phone extension in the bedroom while he dialed John.

When she walked back into the living room after the call, with streaks of mascara running down her cheeks, Luke knew then the song was as mind-blowing as he'd first thought. The lyrics depicted exactly the right emotion and would make a great George Jones tune.

With a little tweaking, it would be the title track for the CD.

Now it was time to get to work.

The next day, Luke called to set up a meeting with Mark and Jerry, and then dialed Darlina to let her know they'd be driving to Abilene as soon as they both got off work.

When he hung up the phone, he let out a long, slow breath. Nothing could squelch the excitement that built in his chest. Finally, after all of the long years, he was going to make a full album. He knew no one called them that anymore, and he'd work on using the new terminology, but what an opportunity life had given him.

He looked around at his outdated cassette and reel-to-reel players and decided it was time to step into the twenty-first century and purchase a CD player. After all, it appeared he was going to need one.

There was one more thing he needed to do. Even though he no longer smoked tobacco, he felt the need to do a ceremony to show gratitude to the Great Spirit for the gift. He strode to the house, gathered Sweetgrass and Sage, and carried them to the backyard. After lighting them both, he waved the smoke in the four directions and silently gave thanks from the depths of his heart. He had lots to be thankful for, but this latest gift that had fallen into his lap, the gift of being allowed to make music again, lifted his soul and spirit. Maybe Darlina was right. Maybe he wasn't complete without making music. A great contentment and peace washed over him. Lucky wasn't a strong enough word to describe what he felt.

***

Returning home that night after the meeting and dinner, Luke glanced over at Darlina. He knew she didn't have any idea of the hard work that lay ahead, but her willingness to sacrifice for this made his throat constrict. He reached across the seat for her hand.

"Unbuckle that damned seatbelt, sugar, and scoot over here close to me."

She grinned. "But, that's against the law, Luke Stone. You wouldn't want me to break the law would you?"

Luke growled, "to hell with any law. I need you as close to me as you can get."

Darlina laughed as she unsnapped the belt and slid easily across the seat.

Luke draped his arm over her shoulders. "Now that's much better." He kissed the top of her head. "Honey, I'm inadequate when it comes to telling you how much your support means to me."

"Oh hush, Luke. I want you to do this project and I'm thrilled about the opportunity."

Luke rubbed her upper arm. "But, you could have said no."

Darlina's reply tore into his heart. "I'd never have said no to such a grand thing, Luke. How could you even think I might?"

Luke sighed. "It's going to be a lot of work and wear and tear on both of us."

"Shh." Darlina put her fingers to Luke's lips. "It'll be fine. I'll simply come home from work every Monday prepared to travel to Abilene. I can pack sandwiches or whatever we need to do. I want this, Luke."

He turned toward her. "Then I want it, too."

***

The following Monday, Luke and Darlina began their weekly trek to Abilene.

It only took a couple of weeks for her to figure out how to prepare food ahead of time, although Luke often didn't eat until after a session.

Late nights, sleepy days when she could barely perform her job, many miles put on the car and a drain on the bank account...and yet it all seemed worth the sacrifice.

Even though Luke had hesitated, the decision to go forward was right. As she always did, Darlina encouraged him to live this dream, reassuring him that she would hold up just fine. If only she could reassure herself that he would do the same.

In spite of failing health, Luke would have a new CD. He explained to Darlina how he'd renew old contacts in Nashville, establish new ones and prepare to make an all-out pitch of his songs.

And if for some reason tomorrow never came, she'd be happy she helped give him this dream.

Luke Stone giving his heart in a performance

Chapter 10

Luke made efforts to reach out and reconnect with artists he'd known in earlier years.

Some of the searches turned into dead ends as so many years had passed, but some he managed to find.

His ears perked up one afternoon, when he heard a DJ announce an upcoming show at the Llano Opry House where two friends from days gone by would be playing.

He picked up the phone and called Darlina.

"Department of Human Services," he heard the familiar lilting voice.

"Hey, Baby, how is your day going? Busy?"

"A little. What's up?"

"Wanna drive over to Llano this weekend to meet a couple of old friends of mine, Johnny Moore and Frankie Miller? They're playing at the Opry house?"

"Of course. Sounds like fun."

"I thought you might. These are two men I worked a lot of shows with back in the 60s. I remember both of them being really good guys."

"I'd love meeting them, honey. I'll talk to you more about it when I get home. Love you."

"Love you more." Luke hung up the phone.

He appreciated the way Darlina moved fluidly with him through whatever transitions he chose. He would enjoy showing off his young beautiful wife to people from his past.

The following Saturday afternoon, Luke and Darlina drove to Brady and surprised Johnny and Frankie at the local radio station where they were being interviewed. They spent the next few hours renewing their friendship and reminiscing about shows they'd worked in the past. It seemed that Luke wasn't the only one who'd dropped off the music scene grid for many years. Both Frankie and Johnny had only recently returned to playing music after a nearly forty year hiatus.

By the time the evening drew to a close, Luke had a promise from both men to stop in Coleman the next day on their way home.

Driving back, Luke talked at length. "Honey, I can't explain to you how it feels to see these guys up there performing. It lights a fire in me but I know I don't want to go back to playing full-time again."

Darlina turned toward Luke. "I totally understand. It was what you did for so many years and you were damn good at it. You know I will support you if you want to start playing more shows."

"That's just it." Luke pulled his cowboy hat off and laid it upside down on the seat beside him. "I don't want to play bars and honkytonks again. Maybe I could do like these guys and play opry shows here and there."

"I'm quite sure you wouldn't have any trouble getting booked. You heard what Tracy Pitcox said today, to let him know when you got ready."

"I know. And we might do that some."

"Lots of these little Opry houses are popping up all around, and you know that the folks at London Hall would be thrilled for you to do a return show there."

"I just feel conflicted, you know? I like the life we've built together and I don't ever want to do anything to screw it up."

"You won't. I believe in you."

He sighed. "You always did, sweetheart, even when I could no longer find one single reason to believe in myself."

***

The following weeks brought even more music renewal when Luke's old friend, Tommy Overstreet, called to say he would be in Abilene for a few days and wanted to come for a visit.

"Do you think you could take at least part of the day off?" Luke asked Darlina when he finished sharing the news.

"Of course I will. I'd love to meet Tommy. I know how special he is to you, but honey, I think I'll be nervous meeting a star like him."

"He is one of the nicest most down-to-earth guys you'll ever run across." Luke paused. "I'll never forget when he came to Leavenworth prison to do a show and didn't have any idea he'd find me there."

Darlina nodded. "The way he really reached out and tried to help us get you paroled was the sign of a true friend."

"He definitely went way above and beyond. Anyway, he'll be here day after tomorrow. I'll try to convince him to stay for dinner."

"I'll arrange my work schedule to be here." Darlina assured him.

***

Luke stepped outside the sign shop when a red pickup rolled into the driveway two days later. He wiped his hands on his blue overalls and waited.

When music icon, Tommy Overstreet, got out of the pickup and slammed the door, Luke strode toward him.

"Man, it's good to see you." He embraced Tommy.

"It's certainly good to see you, brother. And, under much better circumstances than the last time."

Luke chuckled. "You sure got that right. I've been out of prison now for close to sixteen years and never a day goes by that I don't give thanks for my freedom."

Tommy looked around. "I believe you've done well for yourself, Luke."

"I've had a lot of help, Tommy. Let me put my brushes away and I'll show you around the place."

Tommy waited until Luke closed and locked the door to the sign shop, then the two men walked together toward the back yard.

As they walked, Luke pointed out things he'd built, the large garden he tended along with the roses and cactus beds, the numerous buildings and manicured landscape.

They perched on a picnic table in the picturesque back yard shaded by pecan trees that Luke had planted as seedlings, and talked.

That was where they still sat when Darlina walked through the gate sometime later.

Both men stood up as she came toward them.

"Honey, this is Tommy Overstreet. Tommy, this is my whole reason for living, Darlina."

Darlina stretched out her hand to Tommy, but he brushed it away and embraced her. "I've been looking forward to meeting you in person, young lady."

"I've wanted to meet you for a long time too, Tommy. I know how much you mean to Luke."

Luke smiled inwardly as he watched Darlina blush under Tommy's gaze. As hard as she tried not to be, he knew she was a little star struck.

He quickly diverted the conversation away from her and back to the accomplishments they'd made together. He felt nothing but pride for the hard work both he and Darlina had done over the years. Nothing but love and appreciation for her and nothing but gratefulness for the turn life had taken for him.

By the time Tommy departed, he made a promise to come back for another visit next February when he returned to Abilene for the Celebrity Quail Hunt.

Luke and Darlina stood in the doorway of the sign shop until Tommy drove out of sight. He draped his arm across her slender shoulders.

"Sweetheart, you never ever have reason to feel inferior to anyone. I wish I could somehow make you know that. Yes, Tommy Overstreet has had a measure of success in the music business, but he's just a person, and a damned good one at that."

"I know, baby. It's just that I'm not sure of myself sometimes and afraid I'll say or do the wrong thing."

"Bullshit! That could never happen as long as you're being your sweet natural self. Trust me?"

Darlina looked up at him. "Of course."

"Then believe me when I say that you and I are every bit as equal to anyone who might come around here and that includes Willie Nelson."

Darlina's grin widened. "Oh, do you think that might ever happen?"

Luke winked. "You never know. Life seems to be taking me back to the music."

Darlina wrapped her arms around Luke. "And I'm very happy about that."

Luke rested his chin on top of her head. "If you're happy, then I'm thrilled, because that's all I want in life. I don't know if you have any idea how proud it makes me to see you plucking away on the little Gitjo and stepping outside the box to try your hand at writing. You don't give yourself enough credit for the talent you have."

"I don't think I'm very good," Darlina murmured, "but I do enjoy trying. Someday I hope to be good enough to play along with you."

"Sweetheart, if you would trust in yourself, you could do that now."

Arm-in-arm, the two strolled back toward the dream they'd patiently created.

Luke Stone and Tommy Overstreet

Luke Stone, Johnny Moore, Frankie Miller, Tommy Overstreet

Chapter 11

With the arrival of summer, Luke and Darlina continued taking day trips somewhere almost every Sunday in search of new stock for The Saturday Store. When Luke made the suggestion several years ago, he reminded Darlina each trip could be a tax write-off. They'd explored every small town within a hundred and fifty mile radius and often returned with new merchandise to add to the inventory or vinyl records to add to their growing collection. Sunday had long been Luke's favorite day of the week.

He loved exploring with her, talking about any and everything, listening to his favorite music while enjoying the Texas landscape that he proudly called home. It thrilled him when Darlina got excited about a special find or intriguing place they came across. It thrilled him to have freedom and the blue sky above. And it thrilled him to hear the wheels on the asphalt below.

Every aspect of his life flourished - the huge garden he planted each year, their businesses, the new CD recording, but especially and more importantly, their love. He often thought about the words to an old Red Hayes and Jack Rhoads song. *'…the wealthiest person is a pauper sometimes, compared to a man with a satisfied mind…'*

That fit him. He'd been lots of places and done lots of things in his life, but nothing had been as satisfying as the accomplishments he'd made over the past few years with Darlina.

***

Even though Luke tried to wait until Darlina's birthday, his anxiousness to give her the new guitar won out.

So, she came home from work one July evening, to find a guitar case lying on the kitchen table and Luke resting in his recliner.

"Hi, baby. What's this? Did you get yourself a new guitar? It looks small for you."

"Well, smarty-pants, why don't you take a look at it?" He walked into the kitchen.

She unzipped the case and squealed with delight. "Oh my God, Luke! My very own guitar? And it even has my name on it."

She strummed the strings. "And it's in tune." She slung the strap around her neck and boldly played a song while Luke watched with his hand on the back of her neck.

"Well? What do you think?" He asked when the last note rung out.

She gently laid the guitar back on the table and turned into Luke's arms. "I love, love, love it. Thank you, baby." She stood on tiptoes to press her lips to his. "I can't wait to play it some more. I've got to hurry up and get supper."

"Why don't we order something from Noreta's? I don't mind a bit and I know you're anxious to get the feel of it. I wanted the three quarter size for you because it'll fit better and I had it custom-shopped before I picked it up at Hank's."

"Shopped?" She ran her fingers across the surface of the guitar.

"That means it is perfectly balanced, the neck is perfectly straight and everything about it is flawless, just like you. Happy early birthday, darlin'."

She threw her arms around his neck. "Oh baby, I'm far from flawless, but it's the best birthday ever and not even my real one yet."

"I know." Luke grinned. "I couldn't wait any longer to give it to you." To see her excitement was worth anything he ever had to go through. This was his reward.

She quickly called in an order to the local restaurant and Luke went to pick it up while she changed out of her work clothes. He knew she couldn't wait to play the guitar again and wasn't at all surprised to hear the strings ringing when he pulled back into the driveway with their supper.

The minute the table was cleared, Darlina grabbed her new guitar and headed to Nicole's old bedroom to play.

He felt the urge to call Martin. Since he and Stormi had moved to Las Vegas, they had weekly phone conversations. He was the one child who stayed in touch and showed an interest in his father. Once he hung up the phone, Luke reflected over the year so far. It had been good and he was still here to enjoy it. The doctors weren't giving him much hope of a cure for the circulation problem, but he was giving it his best shot.

And he treasured the daily evening ritual when he and Darlina walked arm-in-arm back to the hot tub. They'd even written a couple of songs while relaxing in the warm bubbling water.

Lily seemed happy with Alexander, Nicole was working her butt off to get through law school, and Darlina had taken to playing the guitar like a duck to water. He couldn't ask for more. He knew he had no promises of another tomorrow, as no one does. So, he appreciated each day for the gift it was.

An hour passed before he sauntered into Nicole's bedroom. "Sweetheart, come back in here and play a little while with me."

"Are you sure, Luke? I'm still not very good, but I love my new little guitar. It is completely perfect."

"You're better than you think. You can watch my fingers and follow along."

She walked to the den with Luke and sat across from him with her new guitar slung over her shoulder. He adored the excited twinkle in her pretty blue eyes.

"This one's in C." Luke hit the strings.

"Be nobody's darlin' but mine, love

Be honest, be faithful and kind

And promise me that you will never

Be nobody's darlin' but mine." Luke's eyes locked with Darlina's as he sang. He hoped she could see the love he had for her. In his own clumsy way, he tried every day. The smile that graced her lips said that maybe she knew.

He continued singing, and winked at her when her sweet voice chimed in with a harmony that blended perfectly. Sure, she missed a few chords on the guitar, but he admired her for trying so hard.

Hell, he admired everything about her. He just had to keep finding ways to let her know.

In the days ahead, Luke and Darlina spent every second of their free time with some aspect of writing or playing music. Also, they continued their weekly treks to Abilene to record. Luke loved reviving the old songs he'd enjoyed for years on the honkytonk circuit.

At the same time, both he and Darlina penned new ones.

He was particularly proud of a new song Darlina had written, a protest song about how country music wasn't country anymore. He'd made her promise to sing it at the October party.

He also knew she was stressing about turning fifty in a few weeks and no matter how he tried, he didn't seem able to convince her that she was still the most beautiful little girl in the world to him.

***

Darlina gazed into the mirror, touching the outside of her eyes with her fingertips and scrutinizing the tiny wrinkles that she saw. She would soon be turning fifty. Over half of her life was gone and what had she ever done except be a mother to the girls and love Luke? And both of those were what she'd wanted more than anything. Yet, somehow she had a deep haunting feeling that life was passing her by. How long had it been since she and Luke had done anything that didn't relate to work or their businesses?

It had been very exciting to go to Dallas for Luke to perform at Sons of Hermann Hall.

And it had been exhilarating last October to watch Luke entertain the guests in their backyard, but again, it wasn't unrelated to work or business. Even the Sunday trips revolved around gathering merchandise for their store.

She ran a brush through her hair, gave one last glance into the mirror and turned her back on it. Time to go to work.

When she reached the office, she called her longtime friend, Sally. "I want to go somewhere special for my birthday. I've always wanted to see New Orleans and if I can convince Luke, will you go with us?"

Sally didn't hesitate. "I'd love to. That's one of my favorite places. How about I call Luke and put the idea in his mind as a birthday gift to you?"

"He's already given me my birthday gift and that's another reason I wanted to call. He bought me a brand new guitar and I love it." Darlina didn't try to hide her excitement.

"That's a wonderful gift. I never imagined that you'd play guitar and write songs. I'm so proud of you," Sally paused. "I'll call Luke as soon as we hang up and talk to him about a trip."

"Oh that'd be great! Turning fifty is really affecting me and I don't want to sit here and be depressed. I want to be somewhere new and exciting." Darlina went on to give Sally an update on the recording project. They talked for a while longer. By the time they hung up, she felt sure Luke would be up for a trip to New Orleans.

Excited, she headed down the hallway to Elora's office. Once she shared the New Orleans idea, Elora agreed it would be the perfect way to celebrate a big birthday. How could Luke say no?

She'd approach the subject with him when she got back home.

***

She and Luke sat at the dinner table that evening finishing their meal when Luke pushed his chair back.

"I want us to start a new tradition this year."

"What's that?" She looked up.

"I want us to take a birthday trip every year. August is a big month for us. Not only is it both of our birthdays, but it's also our anniversary month. I've always wanted to see New Orleans. How about we go there? I'm sure Sally would probably come with us and it'd be good for her too. This is a big birthday for you."

Darlina put her hands over her mouth. "You mean it, Luke? I'd love it. Sally's been going there all of her life and knows the ins and outs."

Luke took her hand and pulled her into his lap. "Don't act like you don't already know. Sally called me and it's all arranged, you little sneaky princess."

"Baby, I just didn't want to sit here and turn fifty and be all depressed because I'm getting old."

Luke chuckled. "Honey, have you looked in the mirror lately? You don't look a day older than when I married you. If you're gettin' old, then I'm ancient. You know, I really don't mind being a dinosaur though."

Darlina brushed her fingers across his smooth jaw. "Know what I see when I look at you?"

"A gray-haired broken down old man?"

"I see a handsome rebel country singer who could still get the young chicks worked up and squealin' if he wanted to."

"Angel, the only young chick I'm interested in is you, and if I can get you worked up and squealin', I'm a happy man. You're all I need." He pressed her against him.

She gazed up at him. "To me, you haven't aged and you still excite me."

"Damn, baby! You're makin' this old ticker of mine go nine-ty-to-nothing."

She grinned. "That's my plan. But, it's all true and you still sing just as good as you ever did."

"In the meantime, we have a trip to plan. Let's look at the calendar and see what days you can take off from work."

"I've already requested to have my birthday off, so I'll just put in for the Tuesday and Wednesday after. Will that work?"

"Yep, we can leave after we close the store on Saturday and go to Sally's or else get up early Sunday morning and head out. Gary will be around here to keep things going while we're gone."

Darlina fairly jumped up and down in her excitement. "Oh, I can't wait. This is going to be so much fun. I think we should rest good Saturday night and leave early Sunday morning. I hope you can hold up to the walking, but if not, we'll take a cab or something. We can do this."

"You know me. I'll hang in as long as I can."

"Of course you will. Oh, Luke, I'm so excited about this trip. Thank you. We've never taken a real vacation in all these years." She extracted herself from his arms.

He stood and pushed his chair in. "I love jazz music and what they have in New Orleans is the real deal. And, if I do nothing else, I want to eat my fill of oysters. Did I ever tell you about the time back in the 60s I had the idea to provide live music on the Paddlewheels and Steamboats that ran up and down the Mississippi from New Orleans up to St. Louis, Missouri?"

She nestled her hand in his. "Yes, but tell me again. You were so far ahead of your time."

Luke chuckled. "I suppose it's true. I was so far ahead that I got way behind."

He launched into his tale as they walked into the living room, full of plans, full of excitement and full of hope.

Hope for many more years together.

Hope for Luke's health,

And hope for the music.

12

Chapter 12

Bright and early on Sunday August 20th, Luke and Darlina prepared for the six hour journey to Sally's house in Bossier City, Louisiana.

The clear azure blue sky and brilliant sun magnified Darlina's exhilaration as she packed food into a small ice chest while Luke loaded their luggage. The special travel CDs filled with their favorite music, which Luke had burned a few days ago on his new player, lay beside her purse. She tingled with excitement for the adventure ahead.

In less than fifteen minutes, Luke locked the door and they climbed into the car.

"I made breakfast burritos so whenever we get hungry, we won't have to stop." She buckled her seatbelt.

"Good idea, baby. Besides that, I like your food better anyway." He leaned across the seat and kissed her before buckling his seatbelt. "You ready for a vacation?" He put the car in reverse.

"I've been ready for weeks." Darlina nestled her hand in Luke's.

He pulled onto the highway and headed east. "This is a big year for us, honey. I'm enjoying playing music again and especially to be recording. It was pretty great to get in Texas Monthly Magazine. Our girls are doing good. Nicole has no idea how proud I am of her for having the ambition to go to law school."

"We always wanted them to be successful. Nicole has her struggles. She was very brave to have gone so far away from home, where she knew no one." She adjusted her seat. "If Alexander makes Lily happy, then I am thrilled. He's different, but I will say he's come a long way since the first time Lily brought him home to meet us five years ago."

Luke chuckled, adjusting the cruise control. "Maybe it was my fault that he barely said a word. He had no idea what to expect from an ol' ex-con. But, you're right. As long as he doesn't mistreat Lily, then I can like him."

Darlina snickered. "Between you and Martin, it's a wonder he didn't hightail it a long time ago. When Martin gets a snoot full of Beam in him, he'll say most anything. But, of course he does it with humor."

"That boy's more like me than any of the other kids. It's almost uncanny how much he takes after me, seeing as how I wasn't around much while he was growing up."

"That wasn't your fault. You never ran out on them. The United States Government dragged you away kicking and screaming."

"That's no lie. I didn't go willingly." Luke put on his sunglasses. "Would you find that Waylon CD I made?"

"Of course." Darlina rummaged around until she found it and slipped it into the player.

"I can't wait to get a belly full of fried Oysters, and don't go lookin' at me like that. I know it's not on my diet, but I'm on vacation." He grinned, winking at Darlina.

"I wasn't going to say a word. You deserve anything you want. You've stuck with the diet for five years now and look at what it's added to your life. That Lubbock doctor would be surprised."

"I know. I've thought about going back to see him just to shoot him the bird and let him know he was wrong. He didn't know my stubborn ass or your determination."

Darlina threw back her head and laughed. "I'd like to see his face. If I had any kind of credentials, I'd put out a cook book with all of the recipes I've created. But, with no medical background I don't think I'd be taken seriously."

"I don't know about anybody else, but I know for sure you've saved my life, again."

Sounds of Waylon Jennings filled the car. Darlina kept her hand nestled in Luke's or lying gently on top of his leg as the miles flew by. Conversation flowed easily between them and Darlina marveled at how much they had to say to each other when there were no life distractions. Between full-time jobs, weekend businesses, and weekly trips to Abilene to record, they barely found time to talk.

They reached Sally's house by mid-afternoon to find her waiting with suitcase packed.

"I thought we could go on to New Orleans this afternoon instead of waiting until morning. What do ya'll think?" Sally rushed to hug them.

"I don't know about you girls, but I'd rather rest tonight and leave early in the morning." Luke stretched his back.

"Yes, I think Luke's right, Sally. He has to pace himself and we don't want him to start out on this adventure tired." Darlina rubbed the back of Luke's neck.

"Now don't go thinkin' I can't keep up with you two girls because you're younger. I simply happen to think we'd be better off to wait 'til mornin'."

"Well, I'm with you two, so whatever you want to do is all right with me. I don't have any food made for supper, but we can pick something up," Sally said.

"Don't worry about food, Sally. I have the ice chest packed and I bet we can whip up something after awhile. But for now, I want to get comfortable and open a bottle of wine." Darlina slipped off her shoes. "Luke, are you ready for a Beam and Coke?"

Luke dropped down on the sofa. "Twist my arm and I might say yes." He leaned his head back and closed his eyes.

Darlina caught the glance Sally shot her and she motioned to the kitchen. In hushed tones, she explained that Luke was doing okay, but he wore out easily and was having a lot of leg pain. Sally assured her they would go at his pace in New Orleans.

Over the next two days, the three of them explored every inch of the French Quarter. Often Luke had to stop and rest, so the girls would drag him into the nearest bar.

A trip down the Mississippi River aboard a paddlewheel took them to the Jean LaFitte National Historical Park. Even though Jean LaFitte was a famous pirate, he assisted General Andrew Jackson in defeating the British Army during the Battle of New Orleans.

Darlina knew this interested Luke more than anything they'd seen on Bourbon Street. He had a deep love for history and especially Southern history.

On their last night in the Crescent City, they chose a carriage ride to take them around the French Quarter.

The driver pointed out historic locations and told stories about events that had taken place there. He stopped the carriage at each bar along the route and waiters and waitresses came out to take their orders, and return with drinks.

By the time the tour came to an end, Darlina felt numb and a little tipsy. She could tell from the way Luke chatted with the driver that he was feeling no pain himself.

When the carriage driver discovered that Luke was a music man, he broke out into *Swing Low Sweet Chariot*, and Luke joined with perfect harmony.

She couldn't help but smile. This was truly the man she'd fallen in love with so many years ago. Yes, he was growing older, but so was she and at that moment she couldn't think of anything better than the prospect of spending their golden years together.

Maybe it was the wine, or the magic of the New Orleans night, but for that moment frozen in time, everything was perfect and would last forever. When Luke stopped singing, she put her arm around his neck and drew him down to her. With lips slightly parted, she kissed him as if they'd never kissed before. Her spine tingled and heart lurched when he raised his head, winked and with his crooked grin, set her on fire.

Tears suddenly formed behind her lids as she remembered Luke's prediction that he would most likely die before her and a shiver ran up and down her spine. Even though she knew it was probably true, she couldn't, and didn't want to imagine life without him beside her.

Darlina, Luke and Sally aboard the Cajun Queen

Darlina and Sally on Carriage with Luke looking on.

Chapter 13

N ot long after Luke and Darlina returned from New Orleans, Luke looked up from a sign he was designing to see his old friend, Johnny Moore, walk through the door.

"Hey, man. Come on in." He shoved the sign pattern aside and walked around the table to shake his friend's hand. "How are you, John?"

"I'm doing good. I'm down from Nashville for a few days and if you have the time, I'd like to visit with you."

"I've got a deadline on this sign, but you're more than welcome to visit while I work. Are you down to do a show?"

"No. I'm visiting family. My wife, Susie, came with me and she'd love to meet you and Darlina. I'll be here a couple of weeks so maybe I can bring her over."

Luke picked up a metal straight edge and laid it on top of the pattern. He carefully followed the lines of the letters, transferring the pattern to the board. "That'd be real nice and I know Darlina would love it. How about Saturday?"

"We'll plan on it." Johnny pulled up a chair. "I've got something I want to ask you."

Luke glanced up. "What's that?"

"You remember I'm from Anson?"

"Yes I do. I believe you had several gas stations over there."

"That's right. Well, you know Jeanie C. Riley is my niece and I'm the one that took her to Nashville and broke her into the business."

Luke whistled. "Now that you mention it, somehow I think I remember reading that in a Country Music magazine while I was in prison."

"Well, anyway, we have an annual Johnny Moore Day celebration day coming up and I'd like to invite you to come and play."

Luke looked up. "That sounds good, Johnny. I'd need to talk to Darlina first."

"Of course. There'll be a full band backing you. My nephew is a good lead guitar player and I've got someone on drums, steel, bass and keyboards. It would sure mean a lot to me to share a stage with you again."

"When is it?" Luke resumed drawing.

"Saturday, October 13th."

"That's the day before our fish fry party here. It'd be pushing it. You know I'm not in the best of health."

"How old are you, Luke?"

"I just turned sixty-six."

"I'm a lot older than you, but the Lord has blessed me with good health."

"You always lived pretty clean, Johnny. I blew out my ol' ticker with too much speed and booze and now I pay the price."

Johnny rubbed his forehead. "I liked you back in the day, but you had quite a reputation. I remember I'd hand off bar gigs to you because that wasn't where I wanted to play."

"Yeah, and I'd give you rodeo gigs. You quit the music business in 1964, didn't you?"

"When Jim Reeves died, both me and Frankie Miller quit. Before him, it had been Johnny Horton's death that nearly convinced us to quit. We were on our way to meet Johnny Horton when we heard about his death on the radio. I was driving and I pulled the car off the road. Me and Frankie sat there and cried for about an hour."

Luke sipped from his tea glass. "Johnny Horton was one of the best and I loved Tillman Franks, Horton's manager. Before I got sent to prison, I was next in line behind David Houston to be promoted by Tillman." Luke focused intently on his work. "The last time I remember seeing you and Frankie was in Dallas. We all three played on the Big D Jamboree. Life is a funny thing."

"Yes it is. I've been a blessed man. I made a good living with the service stations. Then, when we moved to Nashville to get Jeannie C. established, we just stayed."

"Remember that show you and I played at Albany where the stage was so high off the ground? Hell, that thing must have been over 15 feet tall. I was careful not to get to close to the edge." Luke chuckled.

"Yes, I remember. That was the tallest stage I'd ever seen. What do you say, Luke, will you play?"

"I'll say yes on one condition. Darlina's never performed on a big stage before. Would you mind if she did a number or two with me?"

Johnny leaned forward. "Of course not. I'd love to have her."

"Then I'll talk to her and let you know, but pretty sure we'll be there."

Johnny slapped his knee. "Thank you, Luke. I really do appreciate it. There are still lots of folks around who remember and will come out to hear you."

"I hope you're right. I sure wouldn't want to disappoint anybody."

Johnny laughed. "No danger of that."

The two men passed time reminiscing and discussing the plight of modern country music. After a few hours, Johnny stood and stretched.

"I better get going. Miss Susie will be wondering where I am. If it's alright, we'll come back over on Saturday."

Luke laid aside his drawing tools. "We'd love it. And I'll talk to Darlina about the show."

They shook hands and Johnny left.

Luke knew Darlina would be excited for him to perform, but could he convince her to get up on stage with him? All he knew was that he'd try.

That evening after supper dishes were cleared away, Luke opened his guitar case and perched on the edge of a chair. "Honey, I had a visitor today."

Darlina folded the kitchen towel and draped it over a hook. "That doesn't surprise me. Who was it?"

"Johnny Moore. He's down from Nashville for a few days visiting family. He'll back on Saturday with his wife, Susie. She wants to meet us."

"That's wonderful, sweetheart. I'd love meeting her." Darlina pulled up a chair across from Luke.

"There's something else. He's asked me to perform as a guest at the annual Johnny Moore Day celebration in Anson on October 13th."

Darlina furrowed her brow. "That's the day before our party. Think we can handle that?"

"I had the same thought. We'll have to get as much done ahead of time as possible. But, I think we can do it. I'm willing to try."

"Then if you are, I am too. I think it's wonderful that he's invited you." She reached for her guitar.

"That's not all. If I get up on that stage, I insist that you get up with me and sing a couple of your songs too."

Darlina chewed on her bottom lip. "Oh Luke, I don't know. I'm prepared to sing here at our fish fry, but I don't know about a big event like that. What if I screw it up?"

Luke laughed out loud as he strummed a C chord on his guitar. "Hell, baby, what if I screw it up? Here's your chance to sing on a big stage. I insist."

"Oh my! We'll have to invite everyone we know. Maybe Nicole can come home from college. I know for sure Lily and Alexander will be here and so will Sally. I'll invite my sister, Leann, and her husband. Maybe Mom can come, and since Claude and Hilda will be here for the party, they can join us."

"Slow down, sugar. Take a breath."

Darlina put her hand over her mouth. "Sorry, baby. I just get excited."

"I love that you get excited. It's one of the many things I adore about you. Let's look at some songs to work on."

The two put their heads together and soon were lost in the music.

After a while, Luke set his guitar back on the stand and stretched his legs out in front of him.

"I think I want to sew some of my Indian beadwork onto that tan jacket I bought at the thrift store the other day for this show. What do you think?"

Darlina put her own guitar on the stand and stood. "I think that's a wonderful idea. I'll wear the sparkly vest we bought in New Orleans." She positioned her legs on either side of Luke and put her hands on his shoulders. She leaned in and he wrapped his arms around her.

"Sweetheart, do you ever really know how much you mean to me and how proud I am of you?"

She murmured against his shoulder. "I think so. But you couldn't be more proud than I am of you. I love that you've come back around to making music. It feels right. It's what you should be doing."

He sighed. "I suppose that's true, although I'd never admit it to anyone but you. Let's head toward the bed. I want to practice pleasing my audience."

Darlina pushed herself up, giggling. "I don't know about any other audience, but you always please this one."

***

Saturday, October 13th arrived with bright sunshine and high hopes as Luke, Darlina and their crew drove toward Anson. The music event was to be held in the high school auditorium and being a very small town, they had no trouble locating it.

Darlina sucked her breath in and steadied her nerves. Why had she ever agreed to do this with Luke? She wasn't good enough to sing on a big stage. Her stomach did flip-flops and spit dried in her throat.

Luke reached for her hand. "You okay?"

She nodded, not trusting her voice.

"Stick with me. You'll do fine." He guided her inside the auditorium.

Darlina couldn't have been more grateful for the show of support they received from family. Not only did Nicole make the effort to come from Colorado, but Sally, Darlina's mom and aunt, along with her sister and brother-in-law made it for the show.

Nicole joined Darlina backstage in a dressing room. "You look great, Mom. You don't look nervous at all."

"Well, that just goes to prove that looks can be deceiving. I'm more nervous than I've ever been in my whole life. Can you help me fasten this necklace?"

Nicole reached for the Beaded Indian necklace that Luke had made for Darlina and fastened it around her mother's neck. "We're all here for you."

"I know and it means the world to me knowing that you guys are all going to be out in the audience."

Nicole kissed her on the cheek. "I've got to get out front. See you when it's all over."

Once Nicole left, Darlina stared long and hard at herself in the mirror. She had to do this. She couldn't let Luke down.

As if reading her thoughts, Luke knocked on the door, and then opened it. "We're just about ready, sweetheart. Let's go stand backstage so we can watch the show."

Darlina placed her trembling hand in Luke's and followed him.

Before long, Johnny Moore introduced Luke. He leaned in, kissed Darlina and said, "I'll call you out on stage when it's time to join me." He slung his guitar over his shoulder and strode out.

Darlina's heart swelled with pride as she watched Luke perform flawlessly like he'd done so many times. She couldn't express how happy it made her.

He sang through three songs, then announced. "I'm going to get my beautiful wife to join me up here and she's going to sing a couple with me." He glanced to where Darlina stood and motioned to her.

She moved as if being pulled by an invisible string, keeping her eyes on Luke. He nodded and winked and began singing *Blue Eyes Crying In The Rain*.

Darlina joined in on the chorus with her harmony. She smiled. This wasn't so bad.

Then after two more songs, Luke addressed the audience. "Now folks, Darlina's going to sing a couple of songs for you. She's a little nervous so give her some encouragement."

The audience applauded and Darlina placed her guitar around her neck and turned to the band. "I do this one in the key of C. It's the Emmylou Harris version of *Two More Bottles of Wine*."

She strummed and began to sing, forcing her voice to steady.

"We came out West together with a common desire
Fever we had might have set the west coast on fire
Two months later got a trouble in mind
'cause my baby moved out and left me behind
But it's alright because it's midnight
And I've got two more bottles of wine."

Somehow she managed to make it through without forgetting any words and only missing a few chords. She breathed a sigh of relief and spoke in the microphone. "Thank you all so much. Like Luke said, it's my first time on a big stage and I've sure got a case of nerves. But, I'm going to do a song I wrote and then I'll get off of here and let a real entertainer up."

She turned again to the band, gave them the chord and began to play and sing.

Once the last chord died out and she walked off the stage to enthusiastic applause, she let out a huge sigh of relief. But, something had happened. She walked a little taller and nothing could wipe the grin off her face. She'd done it! Somehow she knew that she'd never suffer from a lack of confidence again. She felt exhilarated and wasn't prepared for the reception awaiting her once she rejoined Luke and the two of them walked out front.

When someone asked for her autograph, she gazed at Luke with misty eyes. He tried his best to make all of her dreams come true and just when she thought she couldn't love him anymore, he did something to surpass her expectations.

Luke performing in Anson, Texas at the Johnny Moore Day Celebration

Darlina all dressed up for the big stage.

Chapter 14

O n Sunday, October 14th, Luke and Darlina, though weary from the night before, hosted another fish-fry.

Claude and Hilda arrived with not only a gigantic cooler of fresh-caught redfish, but another one full of jumbo shrimp to be grilled.

They rose early and had things well under way before the noon start time. Lily helped Hilda devein the huge pile of shrimp while Luke hung flags along the fence. The American flag, the Rebel battle flag, the Texas flag and the Bonnie Blue flag all fluttered in the breeze. Alexander helped him string pennants from tree branches to the fences and it took on a festive atmosphere. Music blared from the outdoor speakers Luke had mounted on the fence weeks earlier.

Over the year, they'd gathered more tables, chairs, umbrellas and a pop-up awning to provide a larger shaded area and Darlina, with Nicole's help, placed coverings on the tables and wiped down chairs for their guests.

By eleven that morning, folks streamed into the back yard to the smells and sounds of a celebration.

Darlina stopped to wipe a bead of sweat from her brow and count the number of people who all sat talking and eating. Luke joined her and put his arm around her waist.

She looked up at him. "I've counted eighty people so far. Good thing Claude brought more fish this year."

"Word-of-mouth is the best advertisement. Everyone came back from last year and brought folks with them." He shifted his weight from his left leg.

"How are you holding up, honey?" She wrinkled her forehead. "I know that leg is killing you."

"Ah, I'll be alright. I do believe I'll take this opportunity to sit a spell though."

She watched as he moved to the nearest available chair and fell into it. She knew he was tired. The weekly trips to Abilene, then the show last night, on top of preparing for this event, had worn on him.

For a moment, she almost looked forward as a blessing to Wednesday when Luke would once again be hospitalized. She thought about Dr. Robertson's words at their last visit. The disease would only progress, and so far, they hadn't found a cure. Every artery they replaced soon clogged as was the case now. But for today, she put aside those thoughts and focused on the party.

Sally flew past with a full pan of hushpuppies. "You alright, Darlina?" She threw as she hurried past.

"I'm okay, but not too sure about Luke."

Sally stopped and walked back, glancing in Luke's direction. "Yeah, he's looking a little worse for the wear. I'll go see if he'd like me to fix him a drink."

Darlina put her hand on her friend's arm. "Thank you, Sally. You're the best."

"I can't wait to hear you sing again today," Sally said as she turned.

"I'm not nearly as nervous as I was yesterday." Even as she said it, her stomach gave a familiar lurch. She immediately pushed aside and raised her chin. She'd no longer be a victim to insecurity. Luke loved her and she'd proven she could get on stage and sing.

She would've been content to stay in the background and sing harmony with Luke, but he made it clear he wouldn't settle for that. He wanted her front, center and shining. There was a time many years ago she'd wanted that too. But, this was Luke's time to shine and she'd bask in his spotlight for as long as it lasted.

She watched Sally lean over Luke and felt an overwhelming thankfulness in her heart for her good friend.

Once everyone had their plates full of food, Luke strode to the microphone and invited a group of local musicians up to play. Darlina watched as he helped get their instruments plugged in and adjust the sound.

She was most likely the only one present who knew how much Luke was suffering. He could put on a good front.

Their newest friend, Mike, an actor and screenwriter, ambled up beside her. "I'm getting some good film footage here today and the interviews I got yesterday are great. Thank you and Luke for indulging me."

"No, Mike, it is us who should be thanking you. I can't wait to see what all you got on film."

"I know you're worried about Luke, but he seems to be hanging in pretty good."

Darlina forced a smile. "Yes he is. Enjoy the day, Mike, and thanks for being here."

After an hour or so passed, Luke took the stage with his guitar. He invited the musicians on stage to play along with him and sang several of his standard numbers. Darlina watched as the drummer struggled to find Luke's beat. He did, without a doubt, have his own rhythm, but eventually the drummer caught on and managed to stay with him.

Too soon, Luke stopped, asked her to get her guitar and join him. Her heart pounded and she darted through the back door of the house for her guitar. She took time to make sure the strings were in tune before joining Luke.

They sang one of the songs that would be on the new CD, penned by Bill Graham.

Luke's voice rang out.

"You knew what I was right from the start
You knew the way to a country boy's heart
I wagered my freedom expecting to lose
But I came out a winner the night I met you."
Darlina stepped to the microphone and add her harmony.
"The luckiest bet I ever laid down
Wasn't in Ruidoso or Las Vegas town
It was somewhere between bad odds and good news
In white lace and flowers, I bet on you."

Luke winked at her and grinned.

They sang two more numbers, and then motioned to Lily to join them on stage.

Lily, with a voice likened to Patsy Cline, belted out *Walking After Midnight, Blue Moon of Kentucky,* and then *Delta Dawn.*

Darlina reflected on what Luke had said last year about a family band. Her heart swelled with pride.

She only hoped that it wasn't too late. Luke's struggles grew as he lost his health piece by piece and bit by bit. But, she believed in miracles and would never give up hope that he'd be whole again.

As the sun slipped behind the horizon, the guests drifted out humming tunes and smiling.

Once everything was put away and the last dish cleaned, Darlina sat beside Luke while he polished his guitar. Silence was welcome after the day's activities.

She laid a hand on his knee. "This was good, baby. Everyone had such a wonderful time and it was so great to see you relaxed and singing whatever anyone wanted to hear."

Luke chuckled. "Nothing but good feelings…that's what I want for our place. I don't want any negativity to ever enter here. And if it does, I'll politely escort it out the door."

"How can negativity get in when there is nothing but love? After all, love wins."

He stopped, laid his guitar gently in the case and pulled Darlina into his arms. "This is the start of something exceptional. Everyone here today felt it."

She stroked the side of his face. "It's time for good things to happen, sweetheart. I don't know if you have any idea how happy it makes me to see you strumming your guitar every day, singing and writing."

"I think you're fabulous, Darlina Stone, and don't you ever forget it. I tell everyone you are my angel and my reason for drawing another breath."

He tilted her face up and placed his lips on her eyelids letting his kisses trail down her face to the tip of her nose and finally finding her hungry lips.

"Let's call it a day," he said when he came up for air.

"I agree." Darlina stood and pulled Luke to his feet.

Together, they walked from room to room turning out the lights. As they made their way down the narrow hall, Luke thought again of the old song, *Satisfied Mind*.

Even though they didn't have riches, the comfort they found in each other's arms more than made up for the sparse bank account.

Some things money simply couldn't buy.

***

Five a.m. on Wednesday morning found Luke and Darlina in the car on their way to Abilene to check into the hospital.

This time, Dr. Robertson planned to insert stents into the major arteries in the left extremity. He held hope this would provide more blood flow to the legs and eliminate the constant pain Luke endured.

Luke dared to hope for success and relief one more time.

He glanced at Darlina in the breaking dawn. "Here we go again, sweetheart. Time for another 100,000 mile tune-up." Anything was worth a try, in his opinion. As always, Darlina stayed beside him, as he knew she would. He'd lost count of the number of hospital stays. But, it didn't matter. He'd do whatever it took to stick around as long as possible.

Her laugh cheered him. "As long as it gets you more mileage, it'll be worth it."

Funny how her small soft hand always found his and funny how it never failed to comfort. If he could have but one wish, it would be to stay with her through eternity.

And he would, whether in body or spirit. He hoped she understood that.

***

Christmas 2001 drew near and Luke put Christmas lights around each of the four buildings on the property. It took miles of strands, but then he had lots after purchasing barrels of lights from Larry Gatlin's father in Santa Anna. Curly Gatlin had told Luke that Larry had used these lights on his house in Tennessee. And they were blue.

Luke teased Darlina about having a blue Christmas and she'd laughed at his lame joke.

By the end of November, the blue lights were in place. He'd purchased a wooden freight wagon a couple of months back and decided to make a stuffed Santa and attach him to the seat.

The compound took on a warm and inviting Christmas glow.

He was putting the final touches on Santa inside the sign shop when he heard a car pull into the drive. He grumbled to himself. 'Probably somebody wanting to pass the time by looking in the Saturday Store and not buying a damned thing.'

He waited for the visitors to knock on the door, but instead the door opened without a knock.

"Hey Luke," Bill Graham said. "Thought we might find you in here." Two men followed Bill.

Luke walked from behind the work bench. "Sonny, Bill. What in the hell are y'all doin' on the poor side of town?"

Sonny Throckmorton, tall, thin with a full head of white hair, slapped Luke on the back. "Got someone I want you to meet, man."

Bill Graham, not as tall as Sonny, but much thinner, hugged Luke. They'd known each other since Bill was just a boy. His brother, Clyde Graham, played steel with Luke's band for years. Bill had managed to have a very lengthy music career himself playing with the great Glen Campbell, Wanda Jackson and Lacy J. Dalton, to name a few. "We thought we'd grace you with our presence."

"Shit. I don't know if grace would be the right word," Luke joked.

Sonny put his hand on the man's shoulder to his left. "Luke, this is a songwriter friend of mine, Rock Killough."

Rock looked like a stereotypical Irishman with a ruddy complexion, handlebar moustache and shock of reddish-brown hair. His head came to Sonny's shoulder.

He shook hands. "Howdy, Luke. These two have told me lots of stories about you and I've been wanting to come over and swap a few tales myself."

"Hell, they might've told you a bunch of lies, Rock." He grinned wide.

"Maybe. Reckon we'll just have to sort it out. What are you doin' there with ol' St. Nick?" Rock laughed out loud.

Luke instantly liked the man and if Sonny referred to him as a songwriter, he must be a dandy as he knew enough about Sonny Throckmorton to know he didn't use that term loosely.

"Well, I'm gonna perch him on that wagon out front. I'm just about ready to attach him to the seat."

Sonny asked. "Luke, would you mind showing Rock your museum?"

"Of course not. Let's go next door." He reached for his cup. "Can I get you boys anything to drink?"

"Nah. We've got a few beers out in the car."

For the next four hours, the men talked, listened to music, played guitars and drank.

Sonny pointed his finger at Luke. "Twenty years ago when I was working in Nashville, I ran into Bill Graham and he told me stories about you. About how you had a rockabilly band and robbed banks. He said you had a Cadillac convertible with two or three pretty gals in it all the time and you became my hero."

"Shit, Sonny, you've had twenty-one number one songs and you call me your hero?" Luke narrowed his eyes.

"No, I mean it, man. You dared to walk to your own beat and I admired that in you. Still do. Hell, I even thought about robbing a gas station once just to see what it'd feel like. I couldn't do it."

Luke laughed. "I don't recommend that anyone try robbing anything, especially banks. Here, man." Luke passed his guitar to Sonny. "Play my favorite song of yours, *The Way I Am*."

Sonny took the guitar and strummed the strings lightly. "Wish I was down on some blue bayou with a bamboo cane stuck in the sand..."

When he finished, Luke said. "I used to listen to Merle Haggard sing that on a little transistor radio I had in prison and I'd dream about bein' on a creek bank with a red and white bobber going up and down. Then I'd open my eyes and be stuck behind forty foot walls and iron bars. What inspired that one?"

"I don't know. I was just a kid and the lines kept bugging me. We'd be driving down the road for Daddy to go preach somewhere and I'd daydream about it. The lines were always there."

"Well, they're damned good."

By the time the men left that day, Luke had gained a new friend in Rock Killough. The Irishman was sincere and beyond talented, having penned songs recorded by The Oak Ridge Boys, Sammy Kershaw, Hank Jr., Jerry Jeff Walker and Randy Travis.

Luke marveled at the people who passed through his door. Looking back, he realized that it all began with a man filled with curiosity who wanted to write a magazine article about him. He'd always believed he was lucky and damned if it didn't seem to hold true.

Even with nagging health problems and financial woes, things were still coming up roses. He almost chuckled out loud at the irony.

While he sat lost in his thoughts, Darlina walked through the door. The fading sunlight reflected off her long auburn hair and his heart did flip-flops. Lots of men could lay claim to great accomplishments and riches, but he could truthfully say that she was his greatest treasure. He wouldn't trade her for all the others combined.

He had a woman who believed in him, stood beside him and busted her butt to see that he had everything he needed.

He'd call that lucky indeed.

He pulled her into the circle of his arms and buried his face in her hair.

He gave thanks to the Great Spirit for the opportunity to make a CD and have a chance to promote it. More than anything, he wanted to leave Darlina with something to be proud of.

Even better than that, a more comfortable and secure life for her.

His greatest burning desire was to leave behind a lasting legacy that would inspire others. Dare to dream, and then dare to make the dream come true against all odds.

Guests gathered for the fish fry in Luke and Darlina's backyard.

Lily, Darlina, Luke and Nicole at the October party

Luke, Lily and Darlina performing on the makeshift stage

Chapter 15

Darlina sat in the control room of Hank's recording studio, watching Luke through the glass that separated them. She'd seen, with growing concern, that he'd begun having great difficulty breathing. Dr. Robertson referred him to a lung specialist and Luke now carried an inhaler in his pocket and did several nebulizer breathing treatments each day.

She could see him shift from one foot to the other between verses of the song to ward off leg cramps. Would his health hold out long enough to see this project through to completion?

And even though he had a painful, aggravating corn on his left little toe, he tried not to let it slow him down. However, the distinct limp said it all. She knew the excruciating pain that he endured, the nights when he walked the floor as his legs cramped and ached. The many times she'd applied hot towels and rubbed the muscles, trying to coax some circulation back into them. All of this after two bypass surgeries, two stents and two complete rounds of Hyperbaric oxygen treatments.

All the same, he kept his spirits up and moved forward. He had a steely determination to complete this CD, and Darlina supported that one hundred percent. She'd been beyond thrilled when Luke suggested she sing harmony on some of the songs and ecstatic when Mark agreed. To be even a small part of this historic project set her on fire.

She focused her attention back to Luke. The headphones on his ears, eyes closed and giving his heart and soul through the microphone in front of him, caused her eyes to mist.

He sang, "Old enough to be somebody's hero..."

She thought about the discussions they'd had regarding the title of the CD. This song would have been appropriate, but once *Etchings In Stone* was written, it dropped out of the running.

More than anything, Luke feared that he sounded like an old man. How could she convince him when he doubted himself?

Aging was a funny thing. A man's pride resisted all of the things he'd seen in others before him, the drooping skin, watery eyes, trembling voice and tiredness.

Luke Stone refused to become an old man. In spite of the health issues and in spite of the pain he endured daily, a few weeks earlier, when he'd turned sixty-seven, he joked about living to be one hundred.

Darlina only dared to hope that might be true, but deep inside she knew the health problems that plagued him would eventually win. She treasured each day she awoke beside him, and never took for granted the gift of their love. Often during the darkness of night, she'd awaken and check to make sure he still breathed. Maybe it was foolish, but nevertheless it happened.

They'd been making regular treks to Hank's studio for over a year, and the album was taking shape.

Mark estimated that they'd complete it within the next few months, and Luke set a release date for January of 2003.

Darlina appreciated how the musicians who gathered to play on the album invested a large part of themselves in the project. Not only local musicians came, but others from Nashville as well. This would be a class A recording.

Excitement built and even as she watched Luke struggle, nothing could squash the anticipation of having a new state-of-the-art recording of his music. In a few more months, the completed work would be in their hands. She shared Luke's dream of promoting it. Maybe this would be the way her original dream with Luke would come full circle.

She thought back to when they'd first met and how he toured the roads of Texas with his band gathering devoted fans everywhere they went. When he got out of prison, after fifteen long years, she'd dared to hope he would return to the music, but he'd been dead-set on building a home, raising the girls and making a new life that didn't include playing music.

Now here he was in a studio in Abilene, the town where it all began for Luke and Darlina in 1970, cutting a new album.

She would do everything in her power to keep him confident, positive and moving forward. Even if he was in too much pain to do it for himself.

***

As October approached, Luke and Darlina prepared for another fish fry. A call to Uncle Claude sealed it. He assured them that he'd caught enough to feed a small army.

Darlina sat in the living room with Luke on an early September Sunday afternoon. She watched as he applied layers of medicine to the stubborn corn on the side of his toe.

"Why don't you let me make an appointment with a foot doctor for that thing?"

Luke looked up. "I think I'm gonna have to have some help getting rid of it. I don't understand it. I've done the same thing for years and always managed to dissolve them. This time it ain't workin'." He pushed a pillow under his leg. "Let's see if we can get in this week. I'm ready for the damned thing to be gone."

Darlina nodded. "You need to get it taken care of so you can walk normal again."

Luke reached for his iced tea. "Honey, I have a feeling the fish fry will be much bigger this year. Lots of people have said they're coming and bringing others with them."

She opened a spiral notebook. "It's gonna be great and my mom and Aunt Evelyn are coming again this year. They don't want to miss out on the fun we seem to be having down here." Darlina laughed.

Luke grinned. "It makes me happy that Granny wants to be a part of it. Lord knows it took her long enough to come around but I think she truly cares about me now and I certainly care about her and Aunt Evelyn."

"One thing about my mother, she is stubborn and not easily swayed. You had to work at it. But, she and Aunt Evelyn do love music and they both love you."

"John's bringing some musician friends from Kerrville and other pickers are coming from all over. Lots of the ones working with me on the album will be here and they'll bring their families. We should have plenty of music this year, and a by god fiddle for Claude." Luke shifted in his chair, propping his foot up. "Gary's offered to help me put together a makeshift stage out of plywood so that the mic stands will sit level, and I've got a better PA system this year."

"I'm excited, Luke." She jotted more notes in the spiral.

"You're going to get your pretty little ass up and play and sing again this year. I insist. You've gotten lots better over the past year and I want to show you off." Luke winked at her.

"I really look forward to singing some of the new songs I've written. Although, I must confess that singing them in front of a songwriter like Rock Killough sure scares me."

"Darlin', I'm proud of the way you write and I'd tell you if I didn't think they're good. You know me. I'm always honest even if it hurts someone's feelings. So, I want you to sing some of them."

"I really do enjoy writing. Elora tells me that if I start to get nervous singing, to picture everyone naked." Darlina giggled. "Do you have your set list?"

Luke chuckled. "Lord, sugar, I don't know as I'd want to see all those folks naked." He reached for a small pad. "It's right here." He passed it to Darlina. "You've got what it takes. Be proud of your accomplishments."

"I am proud. I just don't know about singing in front of such an accomplished songwriter." She made another note in her spiral. "I'll sing *Another Texas*. Then I'll do a couple more that I feel pretty comfortable with. Lily's been practicing since their last visit. She's made some excellent song choices. The way she rocks *Blue Moon of Kentucky* gets everyone's toes tappin'."

"That girl has a beautiful voice for sure. I wish they lived closer so that we could work more with her."

"She said they're coming down on Thursday so they can help us get everything ready. We will have a couple of nights to practice with her. We should cook barbeque ribs like we did back in the summer. Those were superb and I don't normally even like ribs."

Luke reached for the TV remote. "I'm going to sit here and sleep to the boob tube for a while."

"I'll go in Nicole's bedroom and practice my songs." She stood and reached for her guitar and songbook. Before she left the room, she stopped beside Luke's chair, bent down and kissed him on the forehead. "Get some rest. Tomorrow night we're back in the studio."

He looked up and sighed. "I don't know what I'd do without you, baby."

"You'll never have to find out." She caressed his cheek. "Holler if you need me."

He closed his eyes and nodded.

No matter how hard she tried, she couldn't shake a worry that gnawed at her like a rabid animal. The struggle to make it through the day was increasing for Luke and there didn't appear to be any solution.

She took a deep breath and lost herself in the music. Now she understood how this had been Luke's solace for all the years he was locked in prison. There was magic in the notes and melodies...Soothing magic. Cares and worries could drift away on the chords of a song.

***

Just as they predicted, the October 2002 fish fry turned out bigger than the year before.

Word had spread. Word about good fellowship, good food and word that Luke played and sang even better than before. So, they came from all around and when a head count was done, over a hundred people gathered in their backyard.

Luke connected a CD player, that would hold five at a time, to the outdoor speakers, and they kept them spinning. They even had some rough cuts from the new CD to debut.

Darlina stood beside her mother and looked around at the crowd. Her heart warmed with the laughter and conversation.

For a brief moment, she panicked. She was going to have to get up and play her guitar and sing words she'd written in front of all of them. A glance at the clock told her the music would begin shortly.

Her legs trembled and stomach lurched. What if she froze? She wished with all her heart she had Luke's calm, cool confidence. She took a deep breath and pushed the panic aside. She'd done it once. She could do it again. She squared her shoulders and smiled.

Luke came to where she stood and put his arm around her waist. "Sugar, this is fantastic. Look at everyone." He turned to Darlina's mother. "Granny, are you and Aunt Evelyn doing okay?"

The short graying rotund woman smiled up at Luke. "This is quite a shindig, Luke."

Aunt Evelyn nodded. "And the food is delicious."

"We're thrilled that you ladies made it this year. I know you're going to enjoy hearing Darlina and Lily sing."

"We can't wait." Granny reached for Darlina's hand. "Don't be nervous. They can't bite you."

Darlina giggled. "I know, Mama." She turned toward Luke. "How are you holding up?"

"I'm hangin' in. You about ready to kick this thing off?"

"Baby, don't make me go first. I'll sing with you and Lily. I need to warm up a little."

"Sweetheart, there's not a soul here who doesn't love you and besides that, if you weren't any good, I wouldn't let you get up there." He planted a kiss on her mouth. "So relax. Let's enjoy this good time."

She smiled at him. "I'll do my best, always."

"Come on." He took hold of her hand and they walked toward the stage.

She watched with pride as he slung his Martin over his shoulders and stepped up to enthusiastic applause. By the time he got through two bars, three other musicians made their way up to play with him. Everyone seemed eager to play along with Luke, as it should be.

After half an hour, he turned to Lily who had joined them on the stage. "You ready?"

Lily nodded.

"Folks, I'm gonna step back now and let our daughter, Lily, sing for you. You remember from last year, how amazing her voice is, and I have to tell you that I think it's even better. But, I'll let you decide for yourselves."

He adjusted the microphone stand for Lily and she stepped up and slowly belted out,

"Blue moon of Kentucky keep on shining
Shine on the one that's gone and left you blue
Blue moon of Kentucky keep on shining
Shine on the one that's gone and left you blue."

The music kicked in at a fast tempo. Lily slipped her shoes off and removed the mic from the stand. She had everyone on their feet before she reached the final stanza.

Darlina swelled with pride, and from the grin on Luke's face, she knew he did the same. She spotted her mom and aunt both clapping and tapping their feet. A twinge of regret that Nicole couldn't come from Colorado to be with them flashed across her mind. But, she was busy pursuing her own dreams.

Once Lily completed her set, Luke leaned over to Darlina. "You ready, sugar?"

She nodded, and he announced, "Alright, everyone, I'd like to get Darlina to sing a few tunes she's written for you. Now, she gets a little nervous, so it's up to you to put her at ease."

While Luke talked, Darlina put her guitar strap over her head and stilled her trembling fingers.

With a glance over at her, he said, "Put your hands together for Darlina Stone." He stepped back and Darlina moved forward.

"Y'all don't have any idea how hard it is for me to get up here and sing words that I've written in front of a great songwriter like Mr. Rock Killough, but I'm going to do my best. From the bottom of our hearts, Luke and I thank you for being here today. We hope that you've had enough to eat and are enjoying this good music. That's what this is all about."

She strummed a C chord. "I'm going to start with a song that was one of my daddy's favorites."

She closed her eyes and began.

"The longest train I ever saw
Came down that Georgia line
The engine passed at six o'clock
The cab passed by at nine
In the pines, in the pines
Where the sun never shines
And we shiver when the cold wind blows..."

She turned around in surprise when she heard a fiddle and saw that another musician had joined them. She smiled and strummed her guitar. She relaxed and enjoyed what she was doing.

The reception from the crowd put her at ease and when she announced that she was about to sing something she'd written, everyone applauded.

Taking a deep breath, she opened her mouth and sang,

"I grew up listening to country radio
Merle, Hank and Lefty and others, don't you know
But now I cannot find them
When I tune it to a country show
The lyrics are lame, it's a crying shame
And there ain't no country soul
There must be another Texas and another Tennessee..."

To her surprise, she found a few people in the crowd singing along with her on the second chorus. A glance at Rock brought a smile when he nodded and tapped his toes.

The exhilaration of being on stage was exactly how she remembered. And with Luke and Lily behind her, her confidence grew.

Finally, she was performing music with Luke. Dreams do come true. Then she remembered how she hid her dream from Luke when they met so long ago in Abilene for fear he'd try to make it come true. 1970 now seemed like a lifetime ago.

A lifetime of dreaming.

A lifetime of promises, and

A lifetime of loving Luke Stone.

She strummed on, smiling inwardly and smiling at Luke.

Luke working at Hank's recording studio

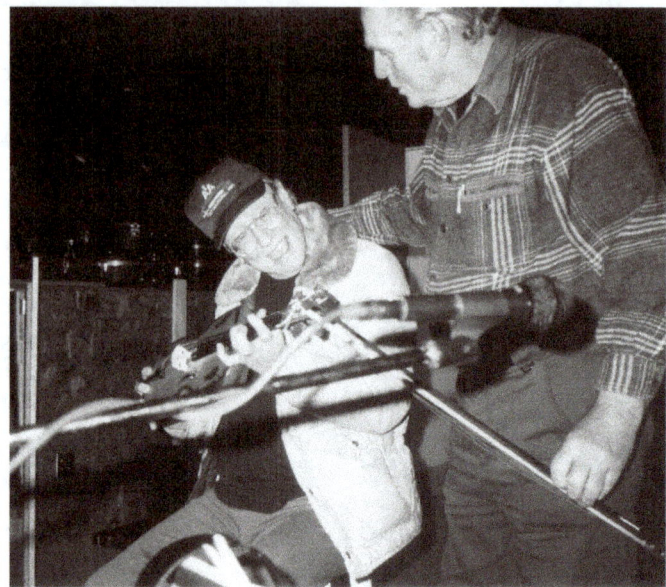

Luke and Bill Graham laying down tracks in the studio

Luke and Darlina enjoying a backyard gathering.

Chapter 16

In the days and weeks following the fish fry, Luke and Darlina continued their routine treks to the recording studio. One piece at a time, the songs were coming together. Luke's goal of releasing the CD in January was in sight as they completed recording all of the tracks and went to the mixdown phase.

Luke had been thrilled when Rock Killough agreed to put piano and harmonica tracks down for him. Then Bill Graham agreed to play fiddle and mandolin. It only added to the list of accomplished musicians who played on the project.

However, a growing problem plagued him. Where the corn had been on his left toe was now a painful wound. He could no longer wear shoes or boots without having irritation and pain. He'd even cut the side out of his shoe to get relief.

Back in September, Darlina had set up an appointment for Luke to see a podiatrist. It turned out the foot doctor underestimated how poor Luke's circulation had gotten in the lower extremities. Once he scooped the corn out with a razor, it created an open wound that now could not heal.

They tried everything, even another round of Hyperbarics, but nothing helped. The tissue around the toe continued to deteriorate and turned into dark colored mush.

Luke watched Darlina's face as she changed the bandage each morning and night. He saw her growing concern when she purchased packages of gauze and bandages at a local pharmacy. It was bad and growing worse.

Luke knew this could not end well. Dammit! If only he could go back. He'd never let the doctor cut on his toe. He had flash-backs to the recurring vision he'd had all of his life, of his left leg being amputated on a civil war battlefield. The agony, the searing pain, the terror was as real as the pain he now endured.

As a last resort, doctors hospitalized him the first week of January 2003 to administer IV antibiotics in hopes of seeing some improvement.

Following more than two weeks of inpatient treatment, lying flat on his back in the hospital bed, Luke Stone stared at the doctor with unseeing eyes. Fear, beyond anything he'd ever felt in this life, knotted in his stomach. It was more akin to terror than fear. He was barely conscious of his tightening grip on Darlina's small hand lying in his own.

"Mr. Stone, we don't have any choice at this point. There is a red streak running up your leg and gangrene is setting in. We have to amputate." The doctor spoke in a firm manner detached from the reality of the news he'd delivered. Words that would change Luke's life forever.

Luke found his voice. "Isn't there *anything* else we can try?"

The doctor shook his head, his voice softening. "We've exhausted our options. The IV antibiotics haven't worked. Hyperbarics and wound care slowed down the progression, but the truth is undeniable. There isn't enough blood flow in the lower extremity to heal it. The bone is sticking through the deteriorated tissue. We have nothing left to try."

Once again, in the recesses of his mind, Luke shuddered as he recalled the dream, nightmare or vision, whatever the hell it was, of the scene on a civil war battlefield. The agony of feeling the saw go through his leg bone was etched into his DNA. Now, here he was facing it again…in this life.

Dr. Shaw said more words and a sob escaped from Darlina's throat, but none of it registered.

He forced himself to look at the doctor's moving lips.

"From the Doppler we ordered yesterday, I can tell you that we'll have to go about six inches above your knee to find enough circulation to heal the amputation. I had hoped to stay below the knee, but there simply isn't enough blood flow." The doctor pulled up a chair. "It's much easier to learn to walk again with a below-the-knee amputation." He cleared his throat. "I know you must both have questions and you may not even know what to ask at this point, but I will certainly try and answer them."

Luke stared past him at a spot on the wall. When he spoke, he knew his voice sounded dull and lifeless. "I reckon there isn't much to say. I wonder if my ticker can make it through surgery."

"Dr. Robertson is working very closely with me and he feels certain your heart is strong enough. Of course, when you undergo anesthesia, you never know."

Luke finally turned to Darlina. "Sugar, do you have any questions?"

Silent tears streamed down her face and her bottom lip quivered. "The first and foremost concern is that Luke make it through surgery. We can worry about everything else after that."

Dr. Shaw nodded. "I agree, Mrs. Stone. But, I can assure you that we have the best team of professionals in the State of Texas here. He is in very good hands."

"I don't doubt that. We appreciate the effort everyone has made. I know you've all done your best." She swiped at her tears with the back of her hand.

Luke turned back to Dr. Shaw. "I don't have any other questions, Doc. Maybe you could leave us alone for a little while."

Dr. Shaw stood. "I'll be back around later tonight to check in on you and let you know when I've scheduled the surgery."

"Thank you."

Once the doctor left the room, Luke turned to Darlina. He scooted to the left side of the bed and patted it beside him. "Get up here with me, sugar."

She blew her nose loudly, slipped off her shoes and slid into the narrow hospital bed. Luke's arm circled her easily and he kissed the top of her head. "You think you can still love a one-legged man?"

"Oh Luke." A whimper left her throat. "I would still love you with no legs. We've never faced anything in life we can't get through, and this will be no different."

He stroked her hair. "I wish I'd realized just how bad the circulation had gotten before I let that damned foot doctor use his razor. He didn't know either."

"None of us knew, sweetheart." She touched his face. "You've endured so much pain."

"Remember the nightmares I used to have where I'd get my leg amputated on a civil war battlefield?"

"Yes."

"Ain't life a funny thing? Maybe that was some sort of premonition or maybe it really did happen in another place and time. At least, I won't feel the saw going through the bone this go 'round."

Darlina snuggled closer to him. Her warmth melted some of the ice that had seeped deep down into his bones.

"I'm so sorry, Luke. I wish I could take away all of your hurt and suffering. I would in a heartbeat."

"I know you would, sweetheart." He sighed. "I don't know what I ever did to deserve you. I guess the Great Spirit knew I'd face lots of hardships in life so he created you to help me."

She turned to face him. "I love you, Luke Stone. I always have and I always will."

They lay in silence for a few minutes, Luke stroking Darlina's back.

Then he began chuckling.

"What in the hell are you finding to laugh about at a time like this?"

"Oh, I don't know. Just irony I guess. My new CD will be arriving any day and here I am turning into a gimp-legged bastard and won't be able to get out and promote it."

"I don't see anything funny about that. We'll do our best to promote it in whatever ways we can. I'm so proud of you for finishing it, honey, and sure glad you got it done before this."

"Yep, me too." He gently brushed her cheek with his left hand which held the IV. "I just don't want to put more hardships on you."

"The biggest hardship you could possibly put on me is to not make it through surgery. So, you tell your heart to keep beating and your lungs to keep breathing for me."

He sighed. "I'll do my best, I promise. Will you call Gary at the sign shop and see if he can drive up? There are some things I need him to do."

"Of course. You know I'll do anything you need." She laid her left arm across his chest.

"I need him to build a couple of ramps going into the house. There's no hurry, 'cause I'll be in here for a while."

"I'm sure he'll be happy to take care of it. Honey, we've had kind of a good life, haven't we?"

"I have lots of regrets, but the biggest is that I haven't been able to provide a big fancy house for you. A princess deserves more than a patched up trailer house."

He felt her smile against his neck. "I don't need a big fancy house. I have regrets too, but mine are that I ever fought with you over anything. Right now, it all seems silly. Forgive me?"

"Darlin', if anyone needs forgiving, it's me. I know I was hard on our little girls, but dammit, I wanted them to grow up to be strong women and you were too soft so I had to be the hard-ass."

"I suppose, but still, I wish I'd done things differently."

"When the boxes of CDs get to the house, I want you to bring an armload up here. All of the nurses have said they want one and Dr. Robertson wants several, so maybe you can sell enough to help with all the extra expense of this shit."

"I will. I'm so anxious to get them. The artwork on the cover was great and I loved that you used your prison number on it."

"That number is forever burned in my DNA. Most folks won't even recognize that it's a prison number. It'll give 'em something to wonder about."

A nurse opened the door and wheeled in the blood pressure machine. "I need to get your vitals, Mr. Stone."

Darlina pushed herself up, kissed Luke and climbed out of the bed.

Thoughts raced through Luke's head and his jaw worked as he tried hard to process them. He'd known this was most likely coming, but to hear the words, put it in a whole different perspective. This was real. This was permanent.

Most of all, he didn't want to make life any harder for Darlina and beyond a doubt, losing a leg would change everything.

Would he still be able to make love to this woman who continually took his breath away? He couldn't bear to think that he wouldn't.

Certainly, he'd have to be done with the sign work. Maybe Gary would carry it on. If not, he'd close the doors.

And then there was the music. How on earth could he promote this CD without taking it to Nashville? He'd reestablished some connections and had planned to take a trip that way as soon as he had it in his hands.

How would he be able to help Darlina make a living? Maybe he could draw some sort of disability. Although, through the years of playing music, he hadn't paid social security and adding the fifteen years he'd been locked in prison the calculation didn't look promising. It wouldn't provide enough.

Would he be able to navigate the narrow hallways of the trailer and get in and out of their tiny bathroom? One thing for certain, he'd need to get the tub removed and a walk-in shower installed.

He'd ask Darlina to contact an old carpenter friend of his and get an estimate.

But, there would be time for all of that later. First of all, he had to get through the surgery.

He closed his eyes and summoned the ancient Medicine Men and Shamans. He'd need all of their help to pull through.

With a fresh morphine shot, he drifted off into a drug-induced sleep. The smell of mesquite wood burning on a camp-fire penetrated his nostrils and the sound of drumming and chanting filled his head.

They'd come. He was safe no matter which way it went.

***

At six o'clock on the morning of January 24th, a nurse brought a wheelchair to Luke's room to transport him downstairs and prep him for surgery.

A drizzling rain had begun to fall sometime in during the night, like silent tears from heaven.

Darlina glanced out the window before she followed Luke. Maybe the sky was crying for her, since she would not allow the tears that clogged her throat and burned behind her eyelids to escape. She had to be strong for Luke.

Even though both of them knew the gravity of the situation, Luke kept up a front, telling jokes and forcing a chuckle or laugh now and then. It was hard to laugh when all she wanted to do was scream, but she knew this was what Luke needed. He'd seen enough tears.

"There must be something seriously wrong with me, honey." He lay on a narrow gurney in the pre-surgery ward.

She forced a grin. "Well, we can agree on that, but I don't know what you're talking about this time."

"I was a crippled kid when I was little, with rheumatic fever. Now, I'm gonna be crippled again as an old man."

"I don't see the humor."

"Guess it's more irony than humor." He put his hand wearily over his eyes.

"There are some people out in the waiting room. If you're up to it, I'll go out and let them come in, one at a time." Darlina straightened the sheet covering him.

"Hell, I didn't know I had a fan club." Luke grinned.

"Well, you do. Don't go anywhere and I'll be right back."

One by one, friends and family came back to have a few words with Luke.

The outpouring of love and support overwhelmed them both. It became obvious that the waiting room would be full of people, people who loved both Luke and Darlina.

Once the last one left, Luke looked at Darlina with tears sparkling in his eyes. "I've been a no-good bastard damned near all of my life. I've been selfish never thinking of others, only taking what I wanted. And now look at the people who have come to be here today." He sighed deeply. "I feel unworthy."

Darlina reached for the hand that wasn't hooked to the IV. "Honey, they love and respect you. And you're more than worthy." She looked up when the curtain parted. Panic gripped her heart choking the air from her lungs.

"Mr. Stone, I'm here to escort you back to surgery. Are you ready?"

"Ready as I'll ever be," Luke said groggily. He clutched at Darlina's hand. "If I don't see you again, just know that I've loved you with everything in me."

She fought to swallow past the lump that constricted her throat. "I know. I'll see you in a little bit." She placed a kiss on his forehead and let her hand drift across his chiseled face once more. "I love you."

She stood until the gurney disappeared from sight, then gathered her purse and walked on stiff, wooden legs to the waiting room, allowing her tears to finally flow.

Luke just had to make it through this surgery. It didn't matter what they had to do to manage afterward. None of that seemed important.

All that mattered was that he kept breathing and his heart continued beating. She whispered a prayer and joined the others in quiet vigil for the man who meant so much to all of them.

Chapter 17

Darlina gripped the Styrofoam coffee cup with both hands, only vaguely hearing the conversation that passed back and forth between the folks who held vigil with her.

They meant well and only wanted to take her mind off Luke, but her mind, heart and soul were in the operating room with him.

She wished for one more kiss, one more caress, and one more night of lovemaking. Please, God, don't let it end yet. Don't let it be over. Don't let me lose him.

They'd had long discussions about how this would change their lives and she knew that it would bring adjustments that they couldn't yet comprehend.

Shortly after receiving the news, he talked about getting a prosthetic and learning to walk immediately. Once again, his steely determination peeked through the doom and gloom.

She didn't allow herself to think beyond this moment; this day.

She smiled and nodded to various comments, but kept her full attention on the doorway between the waiting room and surgical ward.

In less than three hours, the door swung open and a tall slender nurse called out, "Mrs. Stone."

Darlina sprang to her feet. "That's me."

The nurse approached her. "I just wanted to let you know that Mr. Stone is out of surgery and we're taking him to recovery. He did fine and someone will be out to get you once he is awake."

Without thinking, Darlina grasped the nurse's hands. "Oh thank you so much." Unbidden tears rushed to her eyes.

The nurse patted her shoulder, then turned and exited.

Everyone stood with Darlina and took turns hugging her.

"See, I knew everything would turn out alright. Luke Stone's the toughest man I know," John Beam said.

"Thank you so much for being here. It meant the world to me and to Luke." She looked into the faces around her. "And that goes for all of you. We know this will be an uphill battle, but like John said, Luke is the strongest man I know. If anyone can do it, he can and will."

Nods of agreement came.

With moods lightened, the group talked, laughed and joked until the nurse arrived to get Darlina. They said their farewells and she hurried through the doors to find him.

As soon as the nurse opened the door to the large surgical recovery room, Darlina spotted Luke in a bed on the right side of the room. She rushed to his side.

He had oxygen tubes in his nose and several layers of blankets covered him. As soon as she touched his shoulder, he opened his eyes.

Smiling weakly, he brought his left hand from under the covers and grasped hers. "Looks like I made it, sugar."

"Of course you did. I never doubted it for a second." She consciously averted her eyes away from the noticeably missing limb and swallowed a lump. "Everyone said to give you their love. They left before this rain turns into anything worse."

"That was really nice of 'em to stay with you." He closed his eyes and for a moment appeared to drift away.

She put his hand back under the blankets and drew a chair up to his bedside. When he shivered under the mound of covers, she tucked them closer around him. It was freezing cold in the room. Funny how she had no memory of the temperature of the recovery room when she first saw Luke after the open heart surgery fourteen years ago.

She anxiously watched his face and felt relief to see that he didn't appear to be in any pain.

The nurse stepped back to the bed. "He'll drift in and out of sleep for a while, so don't be alarmed."

"He seems really cold," Darlina mentioned.

"I'll bring another heated blanket."

"Thank you." Darlina was thankful she'd thrown an extra sweater into her bag. She pulled it around her shoulders.

After a few minutes, Luke coughed and groaned. Darlina sprang to her feet and put her hand on his forehead.

"Do you need anything, baby?" she asked when he opened his eyes.

He nodded. "A drink of water."

"I'll ask." Darlina waved to gain the nurse's attention.

"How can I help you?" The nurse walked toward her.

"Luke would like a drink of water. Is that possible?"

"I'll bring some ice chips and he can have a few spoonfuls but go easy with them."

Darlina sat by Luke's side over the next few hours while he continued to come out from under the anesthesia.

By the time he was fully awake, they had a room assignment and a hospital aide wheeled him through the halls and up the elevator with Darlina trotting to keep up.

When they transferred him to a bed, Darlina got her first look at the freshly bandaged stump. Her heart froze as reality set in. Even though Luke seemed determined, the fact remained that he might never walk again. Sharp pain pierced her heart.

She hid her face, not letting him see her reaction.

Once the staff left the room, Darlina busied herself putting away their things and adjusting Luke's bed. If she stayed busy, she didn't have to think. She didn't have to ponder what challenges life might hold ahead. However, it didn't matter. The most important thing was that he'd survived.

When she straightened his covers, he took her hand. "Baby, please sit down. You're wearing me out watching you."

"Sorry." She pulled the chair close to the bed. "Do you need anything?"

"Yes." His steady blue eyes found hers.

"I need you."

"Sweetheart, you've got me. I'm right here and not going anywhere."

"I can see the look in your eyes. You're scared. Do you think I'm not?"

She glanced away. "I know you're terrified. We both are."

"When the anesthesia guy was going with me into surgery, of all things, he talked about the Civil War and how amputations were done back then. It was damned weird. He had no way of knowing the connection I had with that."

"How strange. I know something powerful went on today. I don't know how to define or even process it, I just know."

Luke sighed. "Maybe I finally put that piece of Karma behind me for good, whatever it was."

"Maybe." Darlina laid her head on Luke's arm and he freed his other hand from the covers to stroke her hair.

"We're gonna get through this. Don't ever doubt it."

She raised her head. "I won't."

***

Over the next few days, they settled into what promised to be a lengthy hospital stay. Darlina made a trip home to oversee the ramps and shower installation. And she needed to check on the water to make sure no pipes had frozen or burst in the frigid temperatures.

She and Luke also suspected the CDs might have arrived.

Sure enough, Gary had been there for the delivery and locked the boxes inside the sign shop. Darlina eagerly tore into one and held the gold and black CD in her hands, then clutched it to her heart. They'd done it! And they were beautiful. She couldn't wait to take them to Luke and found a small box that would hold twenty.

She carried the remaining boxes to the house and found that Gary had already installed ramps for Luke's return home.

With her mind continuously on getting back to the hospital and to Luke, she lined out the installation of the shower, left a key with the carpenter, gathered clean clothes and headed back to Abilene.

One of the things she'd found waiting for her in the mailbox was a gift from the lady who now worked for her in the Saturday Store. It was a small book titled *Hinds Feet on High Places*.

Darlina thought it curious, but tucked it into her bag. She could use some new reading material for the long hours ahead.

She arrived back at the hospital to find Luke sitting in a wheelchair. She knelt beside him and handed over the *Etchings in Stone* CD.

"Turned out pretty damned good, if I do say so myself." He choked. "Just too bad I won't be able to get out and promote it like I'd planned."

"I think it's beautiful, and we'll do the best we can with it. I stopped by Dr. Robertson's office and he bought ten of them. I think he's almost as excited about it as we are."

Worry clouded Luke's eyes. "I hope we can make back what we have invested in them."

"Don't worry, baby. Everything's going to be fine."

The nurse's aide finished making Luke's bed and rang for assistance to help get him back in it.

Darlina watched with a breaking heart as he leaned on the two women and groaned while he transferred the short distance from the wheelchair to the bed.

As soon as he plopped back on the pillow, he reached for the button that would automatically release another dose of morphine.

He closed his eyes for a minute and then quietly asked Darlina for a report from home. She told him Gary had installed the ramps and that the carpenter would be starting to work on the shower. Gary was keeping the sign business going. She assured him all was well.

With a deep sigh, he gave in to the relief the drug brought.

Once he was comfortable and had drifted off to sleep again, Darlina tiptoed around the room, putting away the rest of her things. She laid a couple of the CDs on the table beside the bed. She wanted Luke to be able to reach them whenever he wanted.

After a quick trip down the hall for coffee, Darlina reached for the new book and curled up in the large chair near Luke's bed. She tucked a soft blanket around her legs.

As she watched Luke's chest rise and fall, a deep sadness enveloped her. How could one person be dealt such hard blows in life and still come out fighting?

He inspired her to keep her own chin up and not let negative thoughts creep in. But nothing stopped her heart from breaking for him. She felt helpless and small.

When she opened the book in her lap, the first page caused her to suck in an audible breath. The main character of the story, Much Afraid, was crippled with her feet so crooked they caused her to limp and stumble as she went about her daily chores. She was trapped in a fearful and negative world, yet she longed to climb the mountain and escape the horrors of the valley. What a lofty goal and what determination she would need. How ironic that this book wound up in her hands at this particular time.

At a time when Luke would need all the strength, determination and will he could muster.

No doubt a message would come through the pages as she read on.

They were in this for the long haul. And it would be the longest and hardest road they'd travelled so far.

Many trials, many tests lay ahead. She didn't know what they would be, but they loomed ahead like the mountain described in the book, steep and tall.

Chapter 18

W ithin a week after Luke's amputation, Darlina returned to work half-days and drove the fifty-two miles back and forth between Coleman and Abilene.

He insisted that she leave in time to get home before dark. He worried that she'd hit a deer, have car trouble or that the roads would ice over. It tore him up inside to watch her do it all over again, day in and day out.

Hell, he hated everything about his predicament and the extra burden it placed on Darlina.

Still, he couldn't stand the idea of not seeing her every day. He often thought about the promise he'd made to never spend a night away from her when they married eighteen years ago. He'd already broken that promise more than he cared to remember. But, all of it was out of his control.

***

Fourteen days had passed since the amputation and they moved Luke from a regular hospital room to the physical therapy floor. Twice a day, a physical therapist came to help him exercise and practice hopping with the aid of a walker.

Glancing at the clock, just after lunch, he knew it was almost time for Darlina to walk through the door. His gaze lingered on the untouched lunch tray that sat on the stand beside his bed. The smell of food nauseated him.

The door swung open and he watched Darlina fling her purse and coat toward the small table in the corner. She leaned over the bed like a fresh ray of sunshine. "Everything go all right today, baby?" she asked.

"I reckon. I can hobble down the hall on a walker twice a day. They tell me that's good."

"What have you eaten today?" She lifted the cover from the plate of food.

"Same as yesterday and the day before and the one before that. Nothing." Irritation swept through him.

"Sweetheart, you're going to have to eat if you ever gain any strength back."

"There is absolutely nothing I want. Hell, they even sent the chef down from the kitchen today. He offered to cook me anything I want. Thing is, I don't want anything. I can't stand the smell of any of it. It's just like when I was in prison."

Darlina brushed his hair back. "I really do understand, but it's been two weeks since the surgery and you haven't eaten a bite."

"I'm wounded and all I want to do is crawl off in the corner and lick my wounds like a wild animal."

Darlina straightened. "I have an idea. I'm going to leave for a few minutes, but I promise I'll be right back."

"Don't go get me a hamburger or anything unless you're going to eat it, because I'm not interested." Luke fought to keep the sharpness out of his voice.

He'd gotten her to go along with him at first, by dumping part of his food tray in the toilet when they brought it, but she soon refused.

"I won't. But, I have an idea. I love you, baby, and we're going to get through this."

Reaching for the TV remote, he sighed. "I know."

What on earth could she be going after? And why couldn't she understand that if he tried to eat anything, he'd puke? It was the greasy Indian in him rising up again. Besides, every ounce of weight he could drop would be helpful when he started trying to walk with a prosthetic.

Flipping the channels, he turned to CNN. Hell, he'd see what was going on in the outside world. Anything to take his mind off where he was.

At least the doctor seemed to think the amputation was healing up well.

Yet, how could he still feel the leg when it wasn't there? They called them phantom pains. Said the body still remembered having the limb even though it was whacked off. The mind was a strange thing, but the pain was real.

He gave a troubled sigh and closed his eyes. If he slept, maybe he could forget. Forget that he was only half a man, forget the burden he placed on his angel and forget the ever present helpless feeling.

In less than twenty minutes, Darlina breezed back through the door with a small grocery bag in hand.

"When I was studying all the nutrition stuff, I learned that yogurt has extremely good bacteria to put in the stomach. So, I picked up some Vanilla yogurt for you to try."

Luke grumbled. "I really don't want it."

It appeared to him that Darlina had suddenly gone deaf, as she pulled open the top to the yogurt and reached in the bag for a plastic spoon. "Just try one bite. That's all I ask. I'll even feed it to you."

Luke reached for the spoon and growled. "You don't have to feed me like a baby. I'm a gimp, not an invalid."

Darlina laughed. "I never thought anything remotely like that, dear."

The first bite felt foreign in his mouth, but it tasted good. Before he knew it, he'd finished off the small carton.

"Honey, you are a genius. You know that, don't you?"

"No. I just knew we had to try something and this is all I could think of. See, sweetheart, sometimes you have to trust me."

Luke reached for her and pulled her down on the bed with him. "You stole my line, princess."

She grinned impishly. "I know."

Snuggling in beside him, she laid her head on his chest. "You need a haircut, baby." She reached up and pushed back his uncombed hair.

"Yeah, I reckon I do. Maybe you could get someone to come up here and cut it."

"I'll see what I can do."

Luke savored the feel of her body next to his. He stroked her back and pulled her closer.

After a few minutes, her breathing deepened and he knew she'd drifted off to sleep. She was exhausted. Again, guilt washed over him.

This was never what he'd intended. This whole experience was much like being back in prison again. He was trapped with only half a body and totally dependent on the one person he craved to take care of. Instead she was taking care of him. How would he ever be able to make it up to her?

***

That evening, as Darlina headed the white Oldsmobile toward Coleman, she found herself thinking about the book again, *Hinds Feet on High Places*.

Throughout the story, the crippled girl climbed the rocky and rough terrain, sometimes only moving a few feet upward in a whole day. Surprisingly, with each small step, her crooked feet straightened out a little and it became easier. Determined, she climbed until she finally reached the top where she found herself whole and filled with joy.

The story was such a parallel to what Luke was going through. Not only Luke, but she as well because what one endured, so did the other.

A melody came into her mind and she hummed it. It wasn't a song she'd ever heard but it was very clear. Then words came. She pulled the car over to the side of the road and dug around in her purse until she found a piece of paper.

She scribbled furiously.

There's a mountain I see rising up in front of me.
And it looks like there's no way around
It's steep and it's tall and I can't see a trail at all
Lord, I hope there'll be someone to catch me if I fall
I've got a long way to go and it's an uphill climb
But, my will is strong and so is my mind
I can make it I know but my steps will be slow
I've got a long way to go, but I can make it I know.

She sat staring at the words without realizing that tears coursed down her cheeks. This song was for Luke and her. There would need to be another verse and she laid the paper and pen on the seat beside her.

She wiped her eyes and blew her nose, then looked to see that the road was clear and pulled back onto it. The words kept coming and she positioned the paper on her leg so that she could scribble them down, glancing back and forth between the road and the paper.

By the time she arrived home, she had written the song. She turned the car off and hurried into the house. She went straight to her guitar where she spent the rest of the evening rewriting words and chords until the song was born.

She couldn't wait to sing it for Luke. She'd carry her guitar with her tomorrow.

One little book sent by a thoughtful person had become a source of hope and inspiration.

***

The next day, Luke was determined to be out of bed when Darlina arrived. He sat in a chair close to a window, watching soft white flurries drift down. Thank God the snow wasn't sticking and the roads were clear. The lunch tray had arrived and he'd managed to eat a few bites.

He waited for his reason for living to come bursting through the door. Surprised to see the guitar case slung across her back, a bounce in her step and excitement on her face, he greeted her. "Hey sugar, you look like a woman I used to know. Real pretty, and boy could she get me stirred up."

After a long tongue-tangling kiss, he took a deep breath. How was it possible to still get tingles and shivers up his spine from her touch after all these years?

"What's up, baby? What's with the guitar and your mood?"

"I wrote a song on the way home yesterday and I want to sing it for you. I won't be loud so I shouldn't disturb anyone."

"The hell with them. You sing as loud as you want."

She opened the guitar case, tuned the strings and began to sing.

He knew his face told it all. Tears misted his eyes and the pride and love he had for this woman swelled his heart to near bursting.

When she finished, she laid the guitar down and came into his arms. "What do you think?"

Luke's voice choked. "It's a beautiful song. You did good, sweetheart. Hell, if you keep going, you're going to wind up being the talented one in the family."

She stroked his face. "Ha. That'll never happen. I'm only a speck in your shadow. I'll never have the talents you do."

"You're right. Instead you'll possess your own."

"Did you eat today?"

"Yes. A few bites, but, I'm glad you left the yogurt with the nurse because that's all that really tastes good."

"See, Luke, it's just like the song. We've got a long way to go, but we can make it. And I'll always be there if you fall."

Luke chuckled. "Sweetheart, if I fall, just make damned sure you're out of the way so I don't crush you."

She silenced his words with soft kisses.

They both looked up when a knock came on the door. Darlina raised herself from Luke's lap.

"Come in," he invited.

The door opened and a nurse's aide with short dark hair and slight build came through. "Mr. Stone, I didn't forget what I promised yesterday. I wanted to wait until your wife was here to help me, but I'm going to shampoo and cut your hair to pay you back for the CD you gave me. By the way, I listened to it on the way home last night and I loved it."

"Sugar, that's awful nice of you." He turned to Darlina. "She told me she used to cut hair for a living before she got interested in nursing, so I asked her if she'd cut mine."

Darlina smiled broadly. "Oh that's wonderful. Thank you so much and yes, I'll be happy to help. I'm so glad you enjoyed Luke's music."

Luke sat back and watched as the two women rigged up a portable shampoo sink made from a plastic trash bag hooked to the back of his wheelchair. They laughed and joked as they worked. Then, with one on each side, they helped him up and onto his walker. He hopped to the chair, sat down and leaned · back while they groomed him.

When the nurse finished, she wheeled Luke over to a mirror. "What do you think?"

"Hell, I think I almost look human again." He beamed up at Darlina. "What do you think?"

Her eyes sparkled as she ran her fingers through his hair. "I think you look ten years younger and as handsome as the day I met you."

With their help, he got back into bed, exhausted from the activity. He wondered if he'd ever have energy again, but if he didn't and he still had Darlina, life would be complete.

***

A few days later, they transferred Luke to a different hospital across town to spend another ten days in an intensive therapy and rehab setting.

By the end of that stay, he felt strong and confident enough to make it at home. He knew it would be a challenge just because of the way the trailer house was laid out, but he could do it. All he needed was one chance.

The day Darlina came to take him home was thrilling for them both. It was now near the middle of March and he'd been away too damn long. He fought the feeling of helplessness as she stood in the small space between the door and wheelchair while he pulled on her shoulder to raise himself up and swivel into the car. Then he watched her fold the wheelchair and struggle to lift it into the trunk. Dammit. Everything from here on would be harder for both of them.

But he would be home. He looked forward to lying on their antique iron black and gold frame bed with Darlina beside him. He needed to love her with an intensity that couldn't be denied. That was all he could focus on. He prayed to God that he didn't disappoint her.

Right now, that was all that mattered.

He didn't say much on the drive. He marveled at the crisp spring green of the trees and the beautiful wildflowers that bloomed beside the road. It was good to be back in the land of the living.

The air smelled sweet and fresh. It had been much too long since he'd smelled anything but medicine and antiseptic.

When they reached Coleman, Darlina hopped out and opened the trunk. Luke watched in the side mirror as she struggled again with the wheelchair. Pain stabbed his heart.

She glanced up and caught him watching. "Don't worry, honey, I'll get better at this. I just have to get it figured out and build up some arm muscles."

He opened the door and swiveled his right leg out as she rolled the chair up to him. "I know you will, but you shouldn't have to have arm muscles. You should get to be a little princess. Before we go in the house, would you mind pushing me around to the back yard?" He pulled up on the door and turned to drop into the wheelchair while she held it steady.

"Of course not. Just don't let me dump you out."

"I won't mind if it's you." He chuckled. "I just want to check on the rose bushes."

He helped all he could to wheel himself across the uneven ground. When he rounded the corner of the trailer, the brilliant beauty of red, yellow and pink roses beginning to open took his breath away. "I made it home in time to see the roses bloom."

"Yes you did, and they bloomed just for us."

The sob strangling in her throat broke his heart. He reached for her hand and lightly kissed her fingertips.

Luke and Darlina back home after the amputation

Chapter 19

Given yet another chance at life, Luke Stone was determined to make the best of it. He could learn to do lots of things from the wheelchair, but more than anything, he was determined to walk.

With a new prosthetic leg made to fit and the zeal of a young colt getting up on wobbly legs, he began daily physical therapy.

As much as Darlina wanted to accompany him, he convinced her that he was capable of taking local senior transportation to the facility and then she could pick him up when she got off work. He desperately needed to feel some semblance of independence.

Her eagerness to help almost irritated him. He had to remind himself that it was only because she cared.

She'd arrive to pick him up as he was finishing his last round of walking. She told him it was important to her, to witness his progress.

The physical therapist assisted Luke in removing the leg and placing it in the bag, then Darlina carried it to the car and helped push Luke's wheelchair with her free hand.

Over and over again, he had the overwhelming feeling of helplessness and the fear of being a burden. It didn't seem fair to him or to Darlina, but as their youngest daughter, Nicole, often said, 'it is what it is.' At least he was alive.

On a hot mid-June day, Luke couldn't complete his rounds of walking. He chided himself while he waited for Darlina. Shit! He reached down and rubbed the quivering calf muscle in the right leg.

As soon as she walked in the door, he wheeled himself toward her with the prosthetic leg lying across his lap. Worry instantly flashed in her eyes.

"Will you help me to the car, sugar?" Luke asked with a growl.

"Of course." Darlina took the prosthetic and helped wheel him outside. Once in the car, she turned to him. "What's wrong, Luke?"

"It's my damn good leg. I'm doing pretty good walking on the artificial one, but the good leg won't hold out. I guess the circulation has gone to hell in it now. Halfway around the course, I got a charley horse and would've fallen flat on my ass if the therapist hadn't been with me."

"Oh honey, maybe it's just the hot weather. Maybe you aren't drinking enough fluids."

He turned to look out the window. "Maybe."

"You can't give up."

"I never give up. I may give out, but not up. I'll try it again tomorrow."

After months of daily therapy, Luke finally had to face the fact that he would never walk again. No matter how much he willed the good leg to work, it was not cooperating. He would spend the rest of his life in a wheelchair.

It seemed that Darlina had an easier time accepting that fact than did he. Or maybe she simply hid her true feelings from him. How could he ever resign himself to being stuck in a damn wheelchair? An invalid. Half a man. Half a husband. Dammit to hell!

And what could he do to help make a living? They'd applied for disability and it had been approved, but he only qualified for a little over four hundred a month. That wouldn't even buy groceries, much less the medicine he had to take.

Gary had chosen to walk away from the sign business and the doors closed. The building sat empty.

Luke did the only thing he knew to do. He stayed busy. He designed a tool he could use from the wheelchair, to dig weeds and manicure the flower beds and cactus beds. They flourished under his constant care.

One afternoon, he was doing just that when a pickup pulled into the driveway. As soon as the couple got out, he recognized them as people he'd gone to school with.

"Hello, Luke," the woman greeted him.

"Hi Sue, Roy. What can I do for y'all?"

"I'm looking for a small building to open my barber shop business back up. Since we've moved just around the corner, we were wondering if you'd be interested in renting out your sign shop."

"I don't know if you could turn it into barber shop, but I'll go get the key and you can see for yourself."

Minutes later, the couple examined the small building and weighed the pros and cons.

Finally they turned to Luke. "What if we agree to pay for the expense of installing the plumbing we'd need, would you let us have the first couple of months rent-free?"

"I reckon I could do that. When do you want to open?"

"The first of next month."

They talked on for a few more minutes and by the time Roy and Sue left, they'd struck a deal.

At least it wouldn't be sitting empty and they'd have a little more money in their pockets. Again, the nagging urge to help make a living churned in his gut.

***

As October neared, Luke questioned whether or not to continue with the annual fish fry.

He knew he couldn't do the physical setup he'd done in prior years. But he hated to end the gathering, and Darlina agreed.

A call to his Uncle Claude settled the dilemma. They would try it one more year. If it became too difficult, it would be the last one.

Assured that enough people had volunteered their services to pull it off, invitations were sent and preparation began.

With a new motorized wheelchair, Luke no longer had to rely on Darlina to push him where he needed to go. At last he didn't feel like such a heavy useless burden.

That, along with the new van Lily and Alexander had helped them purchase, eased life as much as it could, given the circumstances.

Luke prided himself in adhering to the motto, *Always do the best you can with what you have where you are.*

Never before did the saying by Teddy Roosevelt mean more than now.

So, on the first Saturday of October, folks began to gather for the annual music event with Luke and Darlina Stone.

The weather turned cool and cloudy. Luke kept an eye to the sky for the first hint of rain. He didn't want his PA system to get wet, even though he had tarps standing by.

At the first rumble of thunder volunteers sprang into action. Speakers came down faster than they went up and men stacked them inside the storeroom.

Just as they brought in the last piece of equipment, the sky opened up and rain fell in sheets.

Guests who hadn't already made a dash for their cars and home, huddled under umbrellas and awnings while Luke and Darlina tried to decide what to do.

"I've got it," Luke declared. "We'll move everything up front under the two carports. We can set up the music under the smaller carport and chairs under the larger one."

"That's a great idea, Luke." Darlina spread the word and everyone pitched in grabbing chairs and heading for the front.

In less than an hour, the music started back and everyone was out of the weather. Darlina's mother loaded the coffee pot and it quickly became the most popular beverage of the day.

Darlina stood behind Luke's wheelchair with her hand on his shoulder. She did that often, and he never got tired of the comfort her simple gesture brought.

Even though several folks prodded, Luke simply couldn't bring himself to try and sing. His breathing had worsened, and the doctor had added new medications to the daily breathing treatments.

He reached up and patted Darlina's hand. He'd get straightened out. It came down to adjustment and all things considered, they'd done well.

To no one in particular, he nodded and smiled.

When it came time for Darlina and Lily to sing, he positioned himself directly in front of them so he wouldn't miss a note.

With pride he listened and tapped his right foot. Lily had chosen to sing Tennessee Waltz and he fought back tears that threatened, as her voice wrapped around each note like a silken thread. Maybe he should have encouraged her to have a singing career. But, as soon as he had that thought, another took its place. No, she didn't deserve that kind of life. He was happy with what she'd chosen and happy that they could give her at least one venue to use her special gift.

Maybe that alone was enough motivation to continue having this yearly event.

With the cool weather and rain, the party ended early.

That evening as Luke and Darlina sat in the den with Darlina's mother, aunt, Lily and Alexander, Granny pointed to Luke's guitar. "I sure would like to hear you play, Luke."

"Granny, you're probably the only person in the world that could get me to play right now." He maneuvered his chair close to where his guitar sat, raised the arm and tuned.

"What would you like to hear?"

"*Farewell Party* is my favorite. When I die, I want you to play it at my funeral."

He chuckled. "I'm not sure that'd be an appropriate funeral song, but if I'm still around and have anything to say about it, I'll see that it gets played." He strummed the chords and began to sing.

He watched as tears formed in the woman's eyes. Somehow, Luke felt that she knew things she wasn't saying.

***

The next two months flew by in a flash.

Luke struggled with aggravation when he knocked paint off the door frames with his wheelchair.

When Darlina came home from work one afternoon in early November, he had a can of paint and brush in hand. He meticulously moved from scratch to scrape and painted over them.

"Hi, honey." She kissed his cheek.

"It bugs the hell out of me to bump into the walls and mess stuff up, that I worked so hard to build."

"I guess it's all part of the deal. Looks like you're doing a good patch job."

"I wanted to get all of this done before we go to Colorado. It's hard to believe that Nicole is graduating from law school."

"She's a very determined young lady." Darlina stepped through the doorway. "It'll be a great trip and I'm so excited that Sally is going with us. Truthfully, I'm more excited at the prospect of going into Bill Graham's recording studio when we get back and putting down a couple of my songs, especially the one I wrote when you were in the hospital."

Luke paused. "Somebody in this family has to carry on the music. Looks like it'll be you and Lily. I'm pleased with the two songs she chose to record. I wrote both of them way back in the sixties. I'm glad Bill thought to give us scratch tracks for you girls to practice with."

"She's going to do an amazing job. We can practice them in the van on the way to Colorado. I'm happy they're going with us to help drive."

"And Martin called today to say he'll meet us there. I told him you'd get the information to him."

"We're going to need to take warm clothes. We aren't used to Colorado in the winter."

"That's for damned sure, and I've gotten to where I stay cold all the time from the blood thinners. Hell, if I ain't turning into an old man in spite of myself."

"Oh really? Well, I happen to disagree."

He patted her bottom as she squeezed between the wheelchair and the wall. "That's why I love you."

"You love me because I disagree with you?"

He winked. "That and the fact that you snuggle up beside me every night and help keep an old man company."

"I love snuggling beside you every night. But, you know what I miss most these days?"

"No telling. The list could be long."

"I miss you getting in the hot tub with me."

"You don't miss it any more than I do. I'm just glad you finally stopped being stubborn about it and go on without me."

"Well, I don't like it, but I do it. At least that way when I come to bed, I'm all warm when I get under the covers." Her laughter tinkled across the room.

Sudden tears misted Luke's eyes. She never complained or nagged at him. She had more patience than Job. She filled his world with love.

He felt inadequate in returning to her what she deserved.

And yet she stayed steadfast. She was his rock even before he knew he needed one.

Thank God for rocks and Darlina.

Chapter 20

Luke listened to the chatter as he headed the van over Raton Pass in New Mexico.

Thankful that the amputation had been his left leg instead of the right, he felt confident in his ability to drive even though the snow and icy conditions had gradually worsened as they climbed higher up the mountain. Once it reached slippery, no one else wanted the task.

It didn't matter that Nicole's graduation fell in the dead of winter or heat of summer, the importance of the event out-weighed all circumstances. He couldn't help but wish there had been a way to bring his electric wheelchair along. Since it weighed over three hundred pounds, there was no way to lift or secure it.

Darlina sat in the front passenger seat while Sally, Lily and Alexander filled the empty spaces in the back. With everyone's winter gear, Luke's wheelchair, walker and breathing apparatus, the van was loaded to the brim.

As the incline steepened and the road grew more slippery, he was glad to have the extra weight. Slowing down to a crawl, he gripped the wheel firmly with both hands.

Darlina reached across the middle console and laid her hand on his leg. "You doing okay, baby?"

"Yep. As long as I can keep us between the lines, I'm doing good."

"I know you must be tired, but I think driving straight through was the best idea. According to the map, we should be there in another four hours or so."

Luke kept his eyes glued to the road. "I'm sure proud of our baby girl."

"Me too. She's had to work awfully hard to make it and will come out with a ton of student loans, but she should have a degree that'll serve her well."

"She always wanted more than we ever had and I'm glad. I just hope she don't forget her raisin'."

"True. She always had champagne tastes on our beer budget." Darlina laughed. "Maybe she'll be able to make enough money as a lawyer to afford the lifestyle she wants so badly."

Lily spoke from the back. "Mom, would you put on the Eagles CD we brought?"

Darlina turned. "Of course. I'll put on anything y'all want to hear. Do you mind, Luke?"

"I love the Eagles. I wrote a song for them when I was in prison, but haven't been able to get it to them yet."

Sally leaned forward. "If you'll give me a CD with the song on it before I go back home to Caddo Lake, I'll do my best to put it in Don Henley's hands. He owns a bunch of property there and comes in now and then."

"That'd be great, sugar. Remind me when we get home."

Darlina popped the CD into the player and the miles slowly clicked off as *Hotel California* played.

Several hours later, when they reached Keystone resort where their reservation awaited, the entire group was beyond exhausted.

Luke tried to take a deep breath and found his lungs wouldn't expand.

He, Darlina and Sally waited while Lily and Alexander went inside to check in.

"We made it, baby." Darlina reached for his hand. "I'm worn out and I know you must be. After we get unloaded we don't have to do anything else until tomorrow."

"That's a damn good deal 'cause this old man's gone about as far as he can go in one day. I can't breathe worth a shit up here."

"It does get harder in high altitude," Sally said. "I used to come up here skiing, and I would always have a hard time breathing."

Lily and Alexander returned with room keys and directions to the condo they'd secured for the family.

Darlina helped Luke into his wheelchair and pushed him inside while the others unloaded the van. He collapsed onto the sofa and leaned his head back.

"Just take it easy, honey. I'll make you a fresh glass of tea and as soon as we get everything out of the van, we'll go to bed."

Luke nodded. What had he been thinking? Oh yes, he remembered. It was the attitude he'd all of his life that he was invincible and could do anything. Damned if that wasn't changing and he didn't care much for it. He gasped for a breath. Sure wasn't much oxygen to be found up here. He had to hold it together. They'd come for a celebration and he'd be damned if he would be the party pooper.

***

The next day, Lily, Alexander and Sally made plans to ski, and Luke and Darlina explored the resort. Martin would be there by noon and Nicole would drive up to have dinner with the family that evening.

Darlina stayed focused on Luke.

She never wanted to do anything to make him feel less of a man than he already did, so went strictly on his cues. She did admit to herself, she was very happy to see Martin once he arrived because he took over the job of pushing his dad around while they explored the area. She enjoyed walking beside them, listening to their conversation. They shared so many of the same interests and Martin seemed completely at ease with helping his dad.

She began to relax and soak up the beauty of the mountains. She'd never seen anything like this. The closest she'd ever gotten were the times, as a child, they would travel over the mountains at Flagstaff, Arizona on the way to California to see her grandmother and grandfather.

But this scenery was breathtaking. Even though the temperature was below freezing, with the dry air and sun shining brightly, it didn't feel that cold. In the south, when it drops below freezing, it is a wet cold that penetrates deep into the bones. That was the kind she was familiar with.

They covered every inch of the large resort, stopping for coffee and food now and then. Before long, Darlina realized it was time to head back to the condo for the evening meal.

Martin suggested steaks and offered to drive down the road to the only store they'd seen in the area. Luke agreed and insisted on riding with him.

Darlina put together a list and off they went. Alone for the first time in days, she stretched out on the sofa and took in the gorgeous view of the mountains and valley blanketed in a glistening layer of snow. Deep tiredness washed over her and she put her hands over her eyes. Her back hurt, shoulders knotted and arms ached.

It had been a hard trip and her constant vigilance caught up with her. She whispered a prayer of thanks for Martin and closed her eyes.

The next sound she heard was the door opening. She jumped up from the sofa and smoothed her hair.

Soon the room was filled with sounds of laughter, everyone talking at once and piles of wet snow suits. Shortly afterward, Nicole arrived.

Darlina did not miss the emotion on Nicole's face when she leaned down to hug her father. It was her first time to see him since the amputation and she could tell it hit her hard. It was soon covered up with conversation as everyone talked at once.

Darlina dropped down on the sofa next to Luke, nestled her head on his shoulder and intertwined her fingers in his. "This is what it's all about, baby."

He stroked her face. "Yes, it is. Our children are pretty amazing."

***

The next day, they gathered at the University Of Colorado School Of Law to watch Nicole walk across the stage and receive her hard-earned law degree.

Luke fought against emotion when he thought about how hard she'd worked to get to this point. He wished he could've made the journey easier for her. But, she wouldn't be the strong young woman he saw in front of him today if things had been easier.

He had no doubt that she'd make it in life. She had a backbone made of steel, ready opinion and a stubborn streak a mile wide. Not to mention the gift of gab that allowed her to express herself in no uncertain terms.

The tears glistening in Darlina's eyes said she was thinking the same thoughts.

When his gaze caught hers, she managed a tiny smile that simply told him she understood.

A full day of celebration, introductions to Nicole's professors and friends, a feast and gifts drew the monumental event to a close.

Nicole expressed over and again how much it meant to her for everyone to be a part of her big day. She now had a promising life and a hundred watt future ahead.

They'd done it. Now to get back home.

Early the next morning, with the van loaded again, the group began the long trek back. This time, Alexander took the wheel and Luke rode in the passenger seat. The girls sat in the back.

Once they'd passed through Denver and onto open road, Luke turned to Darlina. "Do you girls want to practice your songs? We'll be in the studio tomorrow."

"Let me find the lyric sheets. But, yes, Lily and I need to practice."

As soon as she located the papers, Luke slipped the CD into the player and the music started.

He listened while Lily sang, pausing the CD now and then to make a suggestion. Then he moved on to the music for Darlina's songs.

Again, he made suggestions. "If you both can do that when we get in the studio, these songs are going to be great. Lily, you have such a rich voice. I'd hoped that we could do some things that'd include you with the music, but that was before I became one-legged."

Always the diplomat, Lily responded, "Dad, we can still do stuff. You just have to let me know."

After driving for six hours, everyone clamored to stop for food and to stretch. Alexander pulled into a Chili's parking lot just outside Lubbock.

Lily jumped out and unloaded Luke's wheelchair, then Darlina wheeled him into the restaurant. The hostess pushed two tables together and seated them amidst a large crowd. Luke sat at the end of the table and Alexander at the other end.

Luke set his jaw and looked around, trying to control his weary, frayed nerves. This was not the place for him. The noise level, the waiters and waitresses dashing back and forth along with the blaring music only added to the exhaustion that crept through his bones.

He watched Darlina and Sally chatting away and tapped his fingers on the table. Lily and Alexander had their heads together, talking. Luke felt as if he were a million miles away.

Suddenly, a waiter dashing past bumped into Luke. The jolt startled him and he tried to roll in closer to the table.

"Darlina, am I sticking out in the walkway too far?" he asked.

She looked up briefly. "No, I think you're fine." She went back to her conversation with Sally.

Twice more, the same waiter bumped Luke's chair when he passed by.

The third time, Luke came undone. "Hey," he said loudly.

The waiter turned.

"I tell you what, you sonofabitch, if you bump into me one more time, I'm going to shove you against that back wall and chew your feet off around your ankles."

He heard Darlina gasp. "Luke, honey, calm down."

His eyes flashed. "Calm down? That sonofabitch has been deliberately bumping into me and I don't give a damn if I am a gimp-legged bastard, I'm not going to put up with it."

The waiter whirled around and stomped off to the kitchen.

Complete and total silence came from all around. He could see the flush in Darlina's face and knew he'd embarrassed her, but dammit, he couldn't take any more.

"Everyone go ahead and eat," he growled. He lowered his head and took a bite of his dinner.

Darlina waved to their waitress. "We need some to-go boxes here."

"Just go ahead and eat," Luke said.

"No, honey, we need to get out of here. It's too crowded anyway."

"Suit yourself."

Once back in the van, he took the wheel and Darlina rode on the passenger side. No one spoke for the next several miles.

Finally he turned toward her. "One thing you have to realize and realize it good. Even though I'm crippled, I'm still the same man I was with two legs and I don't and won't take any shit off anyone."

"Okay," she said simply. "I just didn't want you to get so upset and have another heart attack."

"I meant what I told the bastard. I know he kept deliberately bumping into me. I asked you if I was sticking out too far and you said I wasn't."

"You weren't."

"Well, I'm sorry if I embarrassed you and ruined everybody's dinner, but I don't apologize for calling him down."

"I should've been paying more attention."

"No, you're not my keeper. You're my wife. He shouldn't have kept bumping into me. I'm still trying to get used to this one-legged thing and I don't need somebody being rude. Here's another example. Have you noticed, since I lost this leg, anytime we go out to eat, they ask you what I want instead of asking me?"

"I haven't noticed."

"Well I have. The next time one of 'em pulls that, I'm going to say, I'm crippled, not deaf or dumb, and see how they like that."

"Okay, honey. I know you're tired. We all are. Let's just get home."

"That's what I'm trying to do." He reached for the radio button and clicked it on.

He hoped she understood what he was saying. He meant every word. He'd never been able to take crap off of anyone and he wasn't going to start now. No, he couldn't fight 'em anymore like he'd done for most of his adult life, but he could damn sure knock 'em down and run over 'em.

Twenty miles down the road, he started laughing. It started out as a chuckle and turned into a full belly laugh. Before long, everyone in the car was laughing with him.

Darlina turned to him. "Baby, why are we laughing?"

"Did you see the look on that bastard's face when I told him I was going to shove him against the back wall and chew his ankles off if he bumped into me one more time?"

Luke with Nicole, Martin and Lily in Colorado

Luke and Martin in Colorado

Luke with Nicole after she graduated from law school

Chapter 21

Arriving home late that night, Darlina gave a long sigh as she stretched her limbs and helped Luke into the house. The weary travelers headed straight to bed.

The next day, she and Lily practiced their songs once more before they climbed back into the van bound for Brownwood and Bill Graham's recording studio.

In the early 60s, Luke along with Bill's brother, Clyde, who was also Luke's steel player, had built the structure that now housed Bill's studio. It had been Luke's recording studio for many years. History had come full circle.

Luke decided they should record Lily first, since she'd have to return to Dallas the next day.

Darlina could barely contain her excitement. She would record the song she'd been inspired to pen on the road between Abilene and Coleman after Luke's amputation, along with another, *Hate The Sin But, Don't Hate the Sinner*, which she'd written in the hot tub one night.

Darlina watched with fascination as Bill and a talented musician he worked with, Jim Glaspy, rearranged the music to a song Lily would sing. Luke had written *A Million More Just Like Him* as a ballad, but they turned it into an up-tempo bluegrass tune.

How you could take a song and without changing the basic chords, create a totally different sound astounded her.

They didn't leave the studio until midnight, but all four songs were recorded.

And Bill had pushed Darlina to do things with her voice that she didn't know she was capable of. She tingled with excitement.

Lily, of course, had been flawless.

They would soon have girl songs to promote along with Luke's CD on Daralu Records.

***

2003 found Luke, with his typical determination, working alongside Darlina to promote their music through every possible avenue. It wasn't unusual to find them packaging CDs to mail to radio stations, promoters, reviewers, scouts or friends Luke had known through the years.

They reached out to every feasible connection anywhere.

Luke now had a website and often received messages from people who heard and liked his music. He found hope when Darlina located resources on the internet that could be of help.

When Darlina found Luke listed in the West Texas Music Hall of Fame under the category of Rockabilly music, he was pleasantly surprised. He'd known the man in charge of the organization, from many years ago in San Angelo. So, he made contact and renewed the acquaintance. Little did they know that, later that year, Luke would be given a special achievement award from the West Texas Music Hall of Fame.

***

With the barber shop now closed and the sign shop building sitting empty again, he searched his mind for a solution. One evening after supper, Luke tossed an idea at Darlina.

"What do you think about me opening a music store in the sign shop building?" Luke watched her face intently.

"I think that's a great idea, honey. The nearest music store to Coleman is thirty miles away in Brownwood. But, where would we get the money to start a new business?"

"The same way we got the Saturday Store started with discarded inventory from the hardware store downtown. I bet if I talk with Mark and Jerry, I could work some sort of arrangement for them to consign inventory to me. It could be like a satellite store for them."

Darlina perched on her favorite spot, the arm of his chair, and draped her arm across his shoulders. "I think it's a fantastic idea, sweetheart. I know you need something to occupy your time and music is the perfect solution."

Luke stroked her hand. "I'll call them tomorrow. At least it's something I can do from the damn wheelchair. Honey, thank you."

"For what?" She rested her chin on top of his head.

"For not giving up on me." He turned his face upward.

"Never, baby. Never." She placed a kiss on his lips and left butterfly touches along his jaw line.

***

When he approached Mark and Jerry at Hank's with his idea the next day, he instantly had a store. Once again, his hands and mind were occupied. And, it also contributed to the household income.

He felt good about where things headed. He loved to visit with the people who came through the door of Hank's #2 Music Store. Some came to buy a set of strings, some to buy instruments and others simply to sit and listen to his many stories.

His days were full and when there was nothing else to do, he drew or wrote. He revived his passion for pen and ink drawings and kept a clipboard nearby with an ongoing project.

He filled legal tablets with songs, poems and ramblings. By god, he would leave something behind on this earth to make his mark; to prove that he once lived and contributed to society.

Not long after the music store opened, a local Coleman man approached Luke about giving guitar lessons to his young son. He hesitated at first, but the more he thought about it, the more he liked the idea.

He'd never considered himself a great guitar picker, but he could play, had chord charts and knew the fundamentals of making music. Hell, why not teach? He'd spent a lifetime learning and practicing.

So, he put together a lesson plan for beginner guitar students and Darlina created folders for each potential student.

Luke figured by the time he taught them everything he knew about playing music, they'd be ready to move to an advanced level. He was determined to make this business flourish.

***

As the tablets and notebooks began to fill up with new songs, Luke focused his attention on an affordable way to record them. Not only new songs he was writing, but Darlina's as well.

After dinner on a spring evening, they worked together on lyrics Luke had started earlier in the day.

"You see, it's about a draft dodger who's been hiding out in Mexico but he wants to come home." Luke chewed on the worn end of a pen.

Darlina peered over his shoulder. "This is a good line, honey. *They say you weren't a hero but what was in your heart no one will ever know.*"

"It says a lot. Help me rhyme this line. *You've spent a sad and lonely life in sorrow and tears.*"

Darlina pulled up a chair. "What if you said something like, you longed to come home all those years."

"Yeah." Luke scribbled. "The war is over, but still he's trapped in his guilt, yet wanting to come back."

They bounced ideas back and forth for the next half hour or so, until Darlina stood and put her hand on Luke's back. "It's time to relax a little bit, honey. Let's put it up for now."

Luke laid the tablet on the coffee table and wheeled his chair around to the recliner. Over time, he'd accomplished an ease of transferring between the chairs. Once he settled, Darlina took her favorite spot.

He looked up at her. "I've been thinking all day about recording some of these new songs we're writing. I know the recording world has totally changed from thirty years ago, but I've been looking in the catalogs at equipment. Can you hand me the catalog I left laying on the dining room table?"

"Of course." She hopped off the arm of his chair and returned, handing it to him.

He took the catalog, slipped on his reading glasses and thumbed through. "Here." He tapped on a page with a corner turned down. "This setup is reasonably priced. I think we could put together a small studio for very little money."

She peered over his shoulder. "Hmmm. Maybe we could get others to come here to record demos too and make enough to pay for it."

"That's exactly my thinkin'," Luke said.

"If I place the order tonight, it'll be here by the weekend."

"I know I'm a dinosaur with all this new modern stuff, but I know several people who would help. I think you could learn how to operate it. You're good on the computer and that's what it's all come down to."

"It'd be a fun challenge for sure, although I don't know when I'd have time to devote to it. Maybe weekends could turn into lesson time."

"That's something else I thought about today." He looked up at Darlina.

She grinned. "Lord, honey, you sure had a busy day in your head."

"It's all I've got to work with. Hell, my ol' body's about done for, so my mind has to work harder." He slipped an arm around her waist. "A high school girl came into the store today looking for a job. She said she'd done house cleaning with her mother, so I hired her to come this weekend and clean house for you."

Darlina frowned. "I wish you'd talked to me first."

"Why? So you can say you don't need any help? You're a stubborn little girl, Darlina Stone."

"I can't deny that, but I like things done a certain way."

Luke sighed. "I know you do, but, you can train her. Then, you'll have more time for this." He pointed to the catalog.

"Of course, you're right. I'll go place the order. Is there anything you need for the store? Strings? Picks?" She stood.

"Nothing else I can think of." Luke reached for her hand. "Did I remember to tell you how much I love you today?"

Darlina chuckled. "No, you didn't, but I already knew."

***

Within a few days, Luke received the recording equipment and set about putting it together. The building they owned, next door, which also housed his music memorabilia and vinyl record collection, seemed to be the right place for the new studio. He hated that he couldn't crawl up in the attic and run speaker wires himself, but hired the young man who'd been his first guitar student, Denny, to help him.

Denny had become more than a student. In a short period of time, he'd become a part of his and Darlina's home and lives. Luke taught him not only to play guitar, but to paint, build fences, plant cactus and mow the lawn. Truth be known, he might've even taught him to cuss a little and, in Luke Stone style, freely gave advice about females.

And even though Luke continued to battle deteriorating health, having now developed diabetes, he kept going forward. He wouldn't stop until he drew his last breath.

He compared it to how he'd felt when he got out of prison. The drive to build a home for Darlina and the girls had been strong. The drive now to do something with a lifetime of music matched it.

Obsessed with leaving a means to provide for Darlina long after he was gone, he wrote daily.

He didn't have to be a rocket scientist to understand that he was in a race with time.

John Beam, Luke Stone and Tracy Pitcox with Luke and his special recognition award from the West Texas Music Hall of Fame.

Dillon, Luke and Denny (Luke's first two guitar students)

Chapter 22

Darlina had now worked for the Texas Department of Human Services for over fifteen years, and in that time, she'd seen lots of employees come and go.

Besides the deep closeness she had with Elora, she'd made other friendships along the way, and in the summer of 2004, one of those friends, Deb, strolled into Darlina's office and sat down.

"What are you doing, sister?" Deb asked.

"Just giving away the State's money. What's on your mind?"

"I've started dating a guy I want to introduce to Luke. He's pretty deep into the Texas music scene and knows a lot of people. I think Luke should meet him."

"Honey, you know Luke. He'll visit with anyone. Next time your guy is in town, bring him by the house."

"He's coming down this weekend. I just wanted to see if it's okay for us to stop in."

"Of course. We'd love to meet him. You know you don't even have to ask."

Deb leaned on the edge of Darlina's desk. "I'll never be able to thank Luke enough for working with my little boy, teaching him guitar. He needs all the help he can get since his asshole of a dad left."

Darlina nodded. "Luke loves working with the children. He doesn't just teach them to play chords on the guitar, but he talks to them about life. He says if he can make a difference for one young person, then he's doing something worthwhile. I just wish he'd sing again. Since the COPD started, he's pretty much stopped." Darlina sighed and pushed her chair back. "I've got an appointment waiting. Bring your friend by and let him and Luke chew the fat."

Deb stood. "I will."

***

The following Saturday, in response to a knock, Darlina opened the door to find Deb and her friend standing on the porch. A tall man with slightly graying hair and twinkling eyes had an arm wrapped easily around her waist.

Darlina hugged Deb. "Come on in."

"Sister, this is my friend, Corbin Ellis." She turned to Corbin. "This is Darlina, Luke's angel."

"It's nice to meet you," Darlina said. "Deb's told me a lot about you."

Corbin laughed. "Sure hope it was all good."

"Of course it was." Darlina grinned.

Deb took the man's hand and crossed the room to where Luke sat. "Luke, this is my friend, Corb Ellis."

Corbin shook Luke's hand. "Deb's told me a little about you. It's good to meet you, Luke."

Darlina closed the door. Naturally curious about this new boyfriend of Deb's she quickly covered the distance between the two rooms. "Can I offer you guys something to drink?"

Deb shook her head. "We just left the liquor store so I've got a bottle of Wild Turkey in the car. I'll go get it while y'all get acquainted."

"Have a seat, man." Luke motioned to the couch.

Corb settled onto the cushion and leaned back.

Darlina turned to Luke. "Baby, can I freshen your drink?"

Luke nodded and passed his cup to her.

Darlina made a beeline for the kitchen and Deb arrived with the Wild Turkey.

By the time the girls finished preparing cold drinks, the two men were deep into conversation about music and its history. Deb looked at Darlina and grinned.

After an hour or so, Luke turned to Darlina. "Sugar, I'm gettin' a little hungry. Why don't you girls go pick up something for us to munch on?"

"What about the new bar-b-que place down the street?" Darlina stood.

Luke nodded, "That sounds good to me. How about you and Deb, Corb?"

"Y'all don't have to feed us," Deb said.

"Sounds good to me. I'm kinda hungry. Here." Corb pulled out his wallet and handed Deb a twenty dollar bill. "Please let me pay for supper."

Amidst objections from Luke about Corb paying for the meal, the girls took off, promising to return soon.

In the car, Darlina turned to Deb. "This is good for Luke. He needed someone new to tell his stories to."

"I hope Corb might be able to take some of Luke's songs to a Texas artist who will record them."

"That's what we've been working so hard for, but we've been sending everything to Nashville. Maybe we'd have better luck in Texas." She reached laid her hand on Deb's arm. "Thank you for thinking of Luke."

***

When Darlina turned the knob to open the door after they'd returned with food, she froze. Luke was singing.

How Corb got him to do that was a mystery, but her heart danced with joy.

She and Deb exchanged glances and rushed in to find Luke seated in the wheelchair with his guitar. Corb sat across from him leaning forward with his elbows on his knees.

Darlina situated the box of food on the table and went to Luke. She placed her hand on his shoulder, then turned and looked at Corb. "I don't know how you did it, but hearing Luke sing is music to my ears."

Corb took a sip of his whiskey and Coke, leaned back and chuckled. "I asked him to show me his guitar and next thing I knew, we were talking about an old Marty Robbins song and he started singing it."

Luke grinned. "I haven't tried much since I got this damned ol' COPD. I can't get enough air to breathe, much less squeeze out a tune."

"Well, whatever happened, it is sure good to hear you," Deb said.

Tears stung behind her eyelids as Darlina cleared her throat. "Let's eat, and maybe we can convince you to serenade me and Deb, Luke. I'll even throw in some harmony."

Luke patted her bottom. "I can't make any promises, sugar, but I'll take you up on the eatin' part."

Once they'd finished the meal and the table had been cleared, the girls followed the men into the living room. Luke sank back in his recliner, reached for his nebulizer, filled it and turned it on.

In between puffs, he told Corb, "I never dreamed I'd live long enough to be an old man, much less a broken down one-legged bastard that can barely breathe."

Even though he could put up a good front, Darlina knew the blows Luke's ego continued to take, especially, when interacting with an able-bodied man. Her heart broke for him once again.

"You're doing okay," Corb replied. "Like you told me earlier, your motto is to do the best you can, with what you have, where you are. Looks to me like that's what you're doing."

Luke nodded, puffing on the mouthpiece. "And I always will."

Once he finished the breathing treatment, Luke talked about a song from Australia that he proclaimed to be the saddest one ever written.

"I don't know, man, I've heard some pretty sad songs." Corb sipped his drink. "Guess you'll just have to sing it and let me decide."

Luke chuckled and looked at Darlina. "Sugar, will you get my guitar from the den?"

Darlina jumped up. "Of course." She returned in two seconds with the instrument and handed it to Luke, flashing Corb a wide grin.

Luke scooted to the edge of the chair, adjusted the strap and strummed. A second later he sang.

"It's lonesome away from your kinfolks at home
By the campfires at night where the buffalo roam
But there's nothing so lonesome, sad or so drear
Than to sit on the stool in a bar with no beer."

Darlina joined in with harmony on the last line of the verse.

Corb tapped his foot.

Luke continued to sing. When he reached the end of the song, they applauded, laughing.

"Now, why are y'all laughing? I told you, that's the saddest song ever written." Luke took a sip from his cup. "Here's one I bet you've never heard. If I could've had any voice in the world, I would've chosen Wynn Stewart. That little bastard could sing. This is one of his."

"Let's hear it," Corb said.

Luke strummed.

"It's a long, long way to the top of the stairs
To a lone lonely room where nobody cares
It's a long, long way to the street down below
But since I lost you, there's just one way to go."

Darlina gasped when she saw a tear trickle down Corb's cheek and struggled to hold back her own.

Luke kept going.

"My mind won't forget you and the bottle has failed
Our love's like a ship that'll never set sail
I can't live, I won't live without you I know
And I can't turn around now, there's just one way to go."

When the last chord faded, silence filled the room. Corb reached into his back pocket and pulled out a hankie. Darlina swiped her eyes with the back of her hand and Deb sniffed.

Luke cleared his throat. "Now there's a real tear jerker."

Corb's voice shook. "I've never heard that song in my entire life and I thought I'd heard them all. It takes the sad prize for sure."

Luke leaned back in his chair and handed his guitar to Darlina. "That's all I can do."

The girls refreshed the men's drinks and they visited a bit more.

Finally, Corb stood. "I can see you're getting tired. We're going to go, but I really enjoyed meeting you and Darlina." He extended his hand to Luke.

"Come back anytime." Luke said.

"Only if you promise to share some more music with me."

Luke nodded. "I'll do my best."

By the time Corb and Deb left, a friendship had been born.

That night lying in their bed, Luke turned to face Darlina. "I have a feeling I made a real friend today."

Darlina wrapped her arms around Luke. "I think so too, baby. I can't tell you how shocked I was that you played and sang for him."

"He had a genuine interest. I could see there was no bullshit to him."

Darlina sighed. "I wish I knew half as much about music history as you do. I've heard your stories a thousand times, but I still enjoy them. You've had quite a life, Luke Stone."

Luke chuckled and drew her close. "Yes I have. I've done lots of things, seen lots of places and known lots of people, but right here in this little corner of the world with you is where I found exactly what I need."

"I love you." Darlina traced the chiseled lines of his face.

"You do know I'm gonna run out of time one of these days, don't you?"

"Shh. I don't like for you to say things like that."

"I just want you to be prepared." Luke stroked her back.

"I'll never, ever be ready." She sighed and molded her body against his.

No, she refused to think such thoughts. They had today and maybe that was all that mattered.

Luke Stone and Corbin Ellis

Chapter 23

The October party came together that year with lots of help. It thrilled Darlina when several families of Luke's young guitar students pitched in. Also, this year, they would have Corbin's help. Being a road manager for a popular Texas band, he knew the ropes.

No longer was the party a fish fry. Instead, because of the growing number of attendees, it was now a bar-b-que. Along with Luke's help, Darlina seasoned eight briskets at a time and smoked them overnight in the large pit he'd built years before he lost his leg. Then she finished cooking them in the oven the next day.

Together, they figured out a system for doing most everything, but, it was Luke's steely determination to continue this yearly tradition that fueled Darlina's spirit. After all, it was a chance to perform, to sing their new songs and showcase Lily's amazing voice. So, the long hours and physical labor were more than worth the outcome.

Granny, Darlina's mother, turned eighty-seven earlier that year, and back in the summer, underwent surgery to unblock the arteries in her neck, in order to lessen the chances of a stroke. She insisted on coming to the party, and wrangled her nephew into driving her.

Lily and Alexander arrived early to assist with preparations, and Nicole flew in from Colorado.

The original reason for the party, family and friends, seemed especially strong this year.

Luke had been working tirelessly with his young guitar students, and insisted they each perform at least one song. Darlina had never seen him be more proud of any accomplishment. These kids gave him purpose and for that, she was thankful.

A cool front moved through on Sunday morning, October 3, 2004 but the weatherman forecast a clear day. After the rain had surprised them last year, Luke anxiously monitored the skies.

With light jackets on and cups of steaming coffee, the volunteers set about the process of putting tables, chairs, flags, pennants, speakers, and microphones in place.

Luke supervised every detail, wheeling his chair from one to the other.

Darlina watched him out of the corner of her eye, knowing that the cooler weather made it even more of a challenge to breathe.

Corb arrived after finishing up at another Texas music festival in the Texas Hill Country.

By noon, the party got underway with well over one hundred people.

Mr. Gene Fuller, the Texas Guitar man, kicked the music off with his Merle Travis style of playing. Other musicians joined with him: John Beam from Mason, Johnny Way from London, Gilbert Olinger, a local keyboardist, and Sticks, a drummer from Mason.

The music got better every year with seasoned musicians showing up to participate.

Darlina stood in her usual place behind Luke's wheelchair with her hand on his shoulder. She bent down and whispered in his ear. "This is the best one yet."

He reached up and patted her hand, nodding. "I'm a little worried about Granny. She doesn't seem to be feeling very good."

"I know. I feel the same, but she wanted to come. She's so thrilled to see Nicole and Lily. I think she'd have walked to get here." Darlina glanced over at her mother sitting with one hand wrapped around Nicole's and the other around Lily's. Worry settled deep in her gut. Her mother was getting old. Tiredness showed in her eyes and her steps slowed. But like always, she was a trooper and would go the last mile.

Even though Luke didn't perform at this party, he did get on stage with his students, and encouraged them by playing along on his Martin.

That evening, after everything was put away and the last flag folded, the family gathered in the den.

Luke reached for his guitar. "This is for you, Granny. *Fare-well Party*, your favorite."

Granny nodded as he strummed and sang.

"When the last breath of life is gone from my body
And my lips are as cold as the sea..."

Granny wiped tears from her eyes when he finished and her voice trembled. "Thank you, Luke. Remember, you promised me to play that song at my funeral."

"Now, Granny, you're going to be around for a long time. But, I promise you that the song will be played at your request."

Darlina looked at the two, remembering how hard her mother had tried not to like Luke. Nevertheless, he'd proved his worth over the years and she'd come to love him.

She choked back tears. She didn't want to ever lose either of them, but something told her to be prepared.

***

On October 31, 2004, at 6 o'clock in the evening, Darlina answered the phone to her sister, Leanne's frantic voice.

"They think Mom has had a stroke and we're on our way to Jacksonville now. I wanted to let you know."

"We'll get our stuff together and get on the road as quickly as we can. I'm not sure Luke is up to coming tonight, so we may wait until morning."

"Okay. I'll call you as soon as I get there."

"Thank you, Leanne. I love you and y'all please be careful." The phone went dead and Darlina held it a minute longer before hanging it up. A sob strangled her throat as she slowly turned to Luke.

"Mom's had a stroke. Everyone's on their way. Are you up to going tonight?"

Luke sucked in a breath. "If everyone's going to be there, I don't see that there's anything we could do. I'd rather wait until morning, but it's up to you."

"Leanne's going to call me back once she sees Mom. Then we can decide."

"Come here." Luke patted the arm of his chair.

Once Darlina settled, he wrapped his arm around her waist. "She knew when she was here that something was wrong. She told me several times to take care of her girls."

Darlina's tears fell unchecked. "She's nearly ninety years old and I know she's tired, but I'm not ready to lose her."

Luke patted her. "You never will be. I sure wasn't ready to lose my dad, mom or brother, but they went anyway."

"I need to call the girls. They'll be devastated." She pushed herself up from the arm of the chair and grabbed tissues from the box.

After making both calls, she pulled a suitcase out of the closet and threw things in she knew they'd need.

Once she rejoined Luke, they sat in silence staring at the TV without seeing. Three hours later, Darlina jumped when the phone rang.

"It doesn't look good," Leanne's voice faltered. "The doctors say there isn't a whole lot they can do. Her speech is slurred and she's lost the use of the right side of her body. But, she's stable for now. Y'all wait and come tomorrow."

"Please tell her that we love her," Darlina felt as though the air was squeezed from her throat. "If there is any change, call, no matter the time."

"Okay. I love you, sister."

"Love you too, Leanne. See you soon."

Sobbing, she turned to Luke. "She's stable for now, but we need to go tomorrow. It may be our last chance to see her,"

Luke nodded and pulled Darlina into the circle of his arms. She rested her head on his chest, taking comfort in the steady beating of his heart.

***

Early the next morning, Darlina loaded Luke's wheelchair and medical equipment along with their suitcase into the van and they high-tailed it to East Texas. They drove straight to the hospital and even though she fought it, Darlina felt impatient at Luke's slowness. She wanted to run to where her mother lay. But instead, she took deep breaths as she helped Luke into his chair and wheeled him in.

When they entered the room, Granny's eyes lit up. She struggled to speak and showed frustration when the words wouldn't come out right.

Darlina held her hand and kissed her forehead. Her mother, the rock of the family, who had survived the Great Depression, worked in the fields picking cotton and knowing deprivation that would destroy a lesser person, was at the end of her race. Even though she tried to control them, her tears refused to cooperate.

"Don't cry," Granny managed to get out.

"I can't help it, Mama. I owe you so much and I'm sorry I caused you so much grief in life."

Granny raised her left hand and touched Darlina's cheek. "I love you." Even though the words weren't clear, the meaning was.

***

Granny lingered for a couple of weeks and passed on November 14th. As Luke had promised, *Farewell Party* was played at her funeral, despite objections from some of the family.

She left behind a family who loved her and strength that had been passed down through them all.

Darlina and her mother who everyone called Granny

Luke and Darlina 2005

Chapter 24

Luke continued to see Dr. Robertson regularly and was honored when he came to one of their yearly gatherings along with another doctor, who was Luke's general physician, and his wife.

In spite of all odds, Luke moved forward, but he knew that time was against him. He had to help make preparations for Darlina to handle things after he was gone, and doubled his efforts to teach her what he could. He'd avoided saying the words that she didn't want to hear, but nevertheless, he planned and did his best.

She proved to be up to the task of learning the recording program, and Luke thought she did a decent job as a recording engineer. Once again, he felt a deep pride for this woman he called his wife.

They recorded demo records in their small studio, and she mailed them all over the world. Some got a little air play, but that wasn't what Luke was after. He dreamed of lots more. He wanted someone to record one of their tunes and take it up the charts.

Corb visited often. He and Luke not only loved music and its history, but also driving the back country roads around Central West Texas and exploring.

Evenings after work, often found Luke and Darlina busy with projects in their small studio. Weekends were filled with burning CDs, applying the Daralu label he'd designed, and packaging them for the mail on Monday morning. He felt a burning push.

How he wished to be twenty years younger.

***

With a faltering national economy and great slow-down of business, Luke and Darlina made a difficult decision late in 2005, to close the doors to The Saturday Store.

It was a decision that did not come easily and even though Luke knew how much Darlina loved the store, it was costing them much more than it was making. So, they hired a local auctioneer to sell off the inventory for pennies on the dollar. Another chapter in their lives came to a sad close.

***

In March of 2006, Lily and Alexander had their first child, a baby boy named Andrew. Luke loved the way Darlina's face lit up when she held her first grandchild.

It had been many years since Luke had held a tiny baby and he felt clumsy and unsure of himself. But the strength of the love that instantly filled his heart brought tightness to his chest.

He reflected on the circle of life. How it was a revolving door with people being born and people dying. He likened it to the seasons of the year and leaves on the trees. It was a continuous cycle...Death and rebirth.

He remembered a quote from Black Elk. *'The life of a man is a circle from childhood to childhood...'*

Even though he heard the hooting of the owls often in the night bringing comfort and hope, it had been too long since he'd paused to give thanks to the Great Spirit. As he gazed on the innocent face of the newborn baby boy, he felt the familiar sense of gratefulness well up inside his heart.

***

Luke knew deep down inside that time was running out for him. How could he possibly tie up loose ends to make things easier for Darlina once he was gone? He'd worked so hard to gather and accumulate, and for what? Only to leave more of a burden on her?

His vinyl record collection had grown to well over thirty-thousand. At one time, he'd hoped to open a vinyl store, but time wasn't going to allow for that. He actively began to seek a buyer for the collection.

In June of 2006, two young men from Michigan purchased them. It took a semi-truck to haul them, and five teenage boys along with Lily, Alexander and Darlina to load them. Luke had always seen the records as an investment and this time, his hunch paid off. Even though it wasn't the store he'd envisioned, perhaps it would be for the young men buying them.

Now he would focus his attention on the recording studio and expand it to accommodate more local songwriters and bands as they found their way to Daralu to record.

***

Darlina saw the silver in Luke's hair and the wrinkles around his eyes increase daily. And although they'd been in and out of the hospital many times over the past few years with everything from more stents to a pacemaker, she couldn't allow herself to acknowledge that Luke wouldn't live forever.

When he talked openly of dying, she refused to listen. How could she imagine living without him? She couldn't bear the thought.

She stayed busy. The people who came through their doors were many. Darlina often arrived home after a workday to find company, and she never minded setting extra plates at their table.

She knew this was what Luke needed. He needed to feel useful and important. He needed to share his stories, his wisdom and his crazy sense of humor.

Corb had become as much a part of their household as any brother Luke had ever known. Darlina had never seen two men grow so close in such a short period of time. He told her what great pleasure he took in introducing Luke to many of the current Texas artists he knew. Tommy Alverson, Jason Allen, Matt Martindale, Davin James, Kevin Fowler, Aaron Watson, Susan Gibson, Walt Wilkins, Amos Staggs and many more became friends with Luke, and often put their boots under Darlina's table for a home-cooked meal.

She loved the respect each showed Luke, and their patience when they listened to the same story he'd told them last time they visited.

Their house rang with music and laughter and a melding of hearts, both when company came but also when they were alone.

When Luke wrote another new song, she'd listen and sometimes offer a line or two. Or if he'd get stuck, they'd put their heads together and come up with phrases to complete it.

Collaborating with Luke gave her a thrill, especially when he thought she had good ideas.

By now, Luke's song catalog consisted of well over three hundred and probably a hundred more half-started.

Darlina believed in their music, and had written over thirty songs of her own. She was proud of her accomplishments and Luke always bragged about her to anyone who would listen.

So, they moved through their days in what resembled some kind of a dance that could change in a moment's notice.

But, the nights…the nights were the best. Even though they didn't make mad passionate love anymore, the closeness, and the pure devotion they had more than made up for the physical limitations. It seemed that when she thought they couldn't get any closer without crawling inside each other's skin, they did.

Her favorite time of the day was snuggling up next to Luke in bed. She'd lay her head on his shoulder and fall asleep while he watched the evening news. Sometimes she'd hear him turn off the TV and sometimes not. Occasionally, he'd wake her up if someone like Willie Nelson or Merle Haggard appeared on the Letterman show.

Everything he could no longer do physically, he more than made up for with creativity. There was very little he couldn't accomplish if he set his mind to it.

Darlina admired his determination to conquer tasks from his wheelchair. Many times he'd come in the house with sawdust all over it from a building project, or he'd stop at the door and ask her to bring the broom to clean it off before he wheeled into the house.

***

Although never surprised at how Luke's creative mind worked, the latest venture he tackled of building his own custom guitars was one Darlina never expected. As with everything Luke Stone did, these couldn't be ordinary guitars. He had the idea to use round silver mesh screens like the ones you find on the fronts of resonator guitars to create an instrument with a built-in microphone.

She realized he came up with the innovation from his own predicament of being confined to a wheelchair and trying to deal with a microphone.

He cut a hole in the top side of the guitar, installed the mesh screen and then inserted a small condenser microphone inside the body of the instrument. He called them Creative Sound guitars, and soon had orders for them.

Many times, after work or on weekends, she'd help him by holding a piece of the guitar until he got it glued into place. And when his lungs couldn't tolerate the sanding dust even wearing a mask, Darlina did the sanding for him.

One Saturday afternoon, as Darlina ran the small electric sander over the guitar body, she had an idea.

Lowering the mask, she turned to Luke, who sat polishing the neck soon to be attached to the guitar. "Honey, since you are struggling so much with this sanding dust, why don't you find someone who will build the guitar body for you? Then you could add your customization and still come up with the same product."

Luke lowered his own mask. "I hate to admit it, but I think you're right. I don't have much tolerance for the dust at this point. I'll ask around, but in the meantime, I have this one sold, so we gotta keep working. I hate like hell that you have to do this nasty work."

"I really don't mind, but I just think it's time to find an easier way." She turned back to the piece she was sanding. "I'm almost done with this part."

They continued working and before long, they were gluing the pieces together. Darlina forced herself to keep her mind on the work and not chores waiting for her inside the house. At the same time, she hoped Luke would find an easier way to build these instruments.

A few days later, through the owners of Hank's Music Store in Abilene, Luke located a retired Luthier in South Carolina who agreed to build the guitar body for him at a reasonable cost with a promise of quality materials and workmanship.

Even though she'd not minded helping Luke, she felt relieved to have the burden made lighter for both of them.

It was during that year, Luke had to go full-time on oxygen to keep breathing. He preached to all of his young guitar students, the irreversible devastation of smoking cigarettes.

The lung specialist had explained that the lungs were one organ of the body that could never repair itself. So, nearly fifty years of smoking had taken its toll on Luke. In spite of it all, he sang when he could and kept his positive attitude.

***

When Luke decided to construct a covered outdoor stage in their backyard, Darlina didn't question how he was going to do it.

She watched over his shoulder as he drew the plans to scale. It would be quite large, and performers would be protected from the weather. He planned to have it completed in time for the 2007 October party.

He said this was his tribute to Uncle Claude who had started these gatherings and passed away earlier in the year.

Sure enough, by the time the first weekend of October rolled around, Luke had a stage built, wired and partially decorated.

Darlina thought he'd lost his mind when he bought cheap Styrofoam coolers to cut up and make into music notes that he painted. He said they'd endure the outdoor weather.

Long ago, she'd given up trying to get him to slow down. It was obvious that the constant movement kept him going. This would be another big year for the October party. Luke drew a t-shirt logo and Darlina ironed them onto shirts. He designed invitations and she printed and mailed them.

One thing became apparent. Luke Stone enjoyed creating; taking nothing and making something beautiful from it. This was his unique talent and what he did over and over.

Nicole announced that she was bringing a young man she'd recently become engaged to marry, to the October party this year. It would be his first introduction to the family. And he played guitar. Darlina felt certain he'd fit right in.

Funny, how she used to think of these events as a flurry of rushing around getting ready. Now, it was simply part of the routine. Part of the dance. Part of life.

But most of all, if he was having a good day, it meant another opportunity to sing with the love of her life. Another opportunity to sing harmony with Lily and another opportunity to sing the latest songs she'd written.

How she treasured those moments and wished she could store them up for the lean times ahead.

Luke Stone, Tommy Alverson and Amos Staggs

Darlina, Luke and Davin James

Luke and Denny holding Creative Sound Guitars made by Luke

Lily and Alexander with the baby, Andrew

Nicole, Lily, Darlina and Luke performing together

Luke and Darlina enjoying music in Kerrville

Chapter 25

Nicole planned her marriage with Paul to take place in Las Vegas in November 2008. Since Luke's son, Martin and his wife, Stormi, lived there, it seemed to be the most convenient setting for all of their friends and family to come together.

Darlina felt apprehensive about Luke flying, since he now relied on oxygen to help him breathe twenty-four hours a day. However, when they consulted with his lung doctor, she wrote a prescription for a portable tank which they could carry on the airplane.

They'd also purchased a portable electric scooter that broke down into pieces to fit into the back of the van. The airline informed them they could check it as curbside baggage.

So, with everything as prepared as Darlina could get it, they arrived in Las Vegas on November 8th. The wedding was set in a chapel in Caesar's Palace on November 10th.

They'd decided to get a hotel room close to the event for convenience. If Luke needed to rest, they wouldn't be far from the room.

Luke had been willing to escort Nicole down the aisle, although it would seem awkward with the wheelchair, so Martin offered to step in.

As Darlina and Luke got ready on the morning of the wedding, a frantic phone call came from Nicole.

"Mom, can you and Dad be at Caesar's in half an hour? The photographer is here and we need you guys in the pictures."

"We have Andrew, but Alexander will be coming to get him and we'll be there as quick as we can." Darlina turned and relayed the message to Luke.

"I'll get ready first, and then help you into your tux. Maybe we can grab some breakfast once they're finished with the pictures."

Luke picked Andrew up and held him on his lap. "Go ahead and get ready. Me and little guy will hang out."

She hurried to the shower after a glance at the floor-length lavender dress she'd chosen to wear. She would be dressed the way a mother of a beautiful bride should be on her wedding day. Thinking back to Lily's wedding, she remembered how she'd felt underdressed. Not this time.

In less than an hour, they were on the way to Caesar's. Although he'd rested well, Darlina thought Luke looked a little pale. She knew he'd put up a good front for Nicole.

She brushed aside growing concern over his health. This would be another special day in their lives. A day they would gain another son-in-law and their baby daughter would have someone to love and cherish her.

Once they arrived, it became apparent there was no need for their presence. Twice, Darlina asked if maybe she and Luke could take the baby and go get breakfast, but each time, was told the photographer would be ready any minute.

The hours flew by and it was time for the wedding to begin and still they'd not eaten. Martin and Stormi's teenage son, Jake, served as an usher. He removed a chair so that Luke could park his scooter next to Darlina in the front row.

The music began and everyone stood except for Luke. Darlina kept a hand on his shoulder, hoping he wouldn't feel out of place.

Her breath caught in her throat when Nicole entered the chapel. With her blonde hair piled high, a flowing white dress decorated with sequins, beads and pearls, filmy veil and bare shoulders, she was a radiant, glowing bride.

Once they were seated, she saw Luke fumbling in his pocket for a hankie. She kept her hand on his arm until he took her fingers and wrapped them in his own.

To make the ceremony more special, Nicole had written a tribute to Granny and asked her best friend to read it.

All of it brought tears to Darlina's eyes and Luke passed his hankie over to her with a wink twice before the ceremony ended.

By the time Nicole and Paul exchanged final vows and everyone filed out, it neared early afternoon.

Luke leaned across to Darlina. "Honey, I'm really feeling faint. I need something with some sugar in it."

She ran to Nicole's dressing room in a panic and found two cookies. Then she rushed back to Luke. "We never got to eat breakfast. I'm sure your blood sugar has bottomed out."

His eyes sunk back in his head in contrast to the paleness of his skin and his hand trembled when he accepted them. "Yeah. I've gone too long without anything. I'm not going to last much longer without something to eat. I don't want to embarrass Nicole by falling out."

Darlina put a reassuring hand on his shoulder. "We'll leave if we need to and get you some food. Maybe these cookies will hold you over until the reception. It can't be that much longer."

He nodded.

The photographer called the wedding party and family together and snapped more photos. Darlina hoped Luke wouldn't look as miserable as he felt.

Lily sang *At Last* during Nicole's reception and Darlina shed more happy tears. Her daughter's beautiful voice sent shivers down her spine and the hairs on her arms stood on end.

Finally, Luke had food. The color began to come back into his face but he was tired.

As soon as the reception wound down, they headed to the hotel room to rest for the trip back home.

Now, both of their daughters were married, successful and making their own way in the world, just the way Luke had always said they would.

Once they were settled back in the room, Luke patted the bed beside him. "Come here, sweetheart."

"Let me hang this fancy dress up and I'll be right there." She slipped the lavender dress onto a hanger and secured it, then nestled beside Luke on the bed.

He stroked her hair. "I'm a happy man right now, honey. I always hoped I'd live long enough to see our girls grown and married. And the baby is a sweetheart. I'm sure there will be many more grandbabies over the years to come."

Darlina turned her face upward. "Andrew is such a special little boy. I never thought I could love any child more than my own girls, but grandbabies are different. It's a different kind of love."

Luke closed his eyes. "They'll help fill a void for you when I'm gone. Always stay close to the girls."

"Honey, I hate it when you talk this way. You aren't going anywhere. You can enjoy all of the grandbabies with me."

He sighed. "Maybe so. I can't say. All I'm trying to get across to you is how important it'll be for you to stay close to the girls."

Darlina sniffed. "I will. I promise." She shifted on the bed. "Now, that's enough sad talk. How about me and you go downstairs to the Casino and drop a few quarters? Are you up to it?"

"I think I could manage that. I'd like a stiff drink about now anyway." He slid to the edge of the bed and put his shoe on.

Within minutes they were engulfed in the dinging of slot machines and sounds of people talking and laughing. It made for a good distraction.

***

In late January, 2009, Darlina arrived home from work on Friday evening, to find Luke giving a guitar lesson in the music store.

"Honey, I've got something to show you when I get to the house." He handed the money bag to her. "I'm almost finished here and I'll be right in."

She took the zippered bag, kissed him on the forehead and went to the trailer to start supper. What could Luke have to show her? Perhaps a new song, poem or drawing?

With leftover turkey enchiladas in the oven, she changed clothes. By the time she came back to the living room, Luke was transferring from his wheelchair to the recliner.

"What do you have to show me, baby?" She perched on the arm of his chair.

Luke pulled down the sock on his right foot. "Look at this. Ever seen anything like it?"

A blister about the size of a small egg protruded on the front lower part of his leg. She sucked in a breath. "No, I haven't. It almost looks like a burn. Did you get too close to the fire?"

"Nope. It just started coming up this afternoon and seems to be getting bigger. Looks like it's full of water. Think maybe we should pop it?"

"Oh, I'd be afraid to, Luke. I think I better call and get you an appointment with the doc." She leaned down to get a closer look. The all too vivid memory of a small corn that ended with Luke's amputation crushed against her chest. Surely this would not be a repeat of that horrific event.

"Yeah, I think so too, but you won't be able to reach him until Monday. There is no way to get in over the weekend and I don't think this is anything that would require going to the emergency room."

"Maybe not, but we'll keep a close watch on it. I can't imagine what on earth it could be. It just looks like fluid under the skin. Does it hurt?"

"I can't feel a thing. This is crazy shit. Maybe it'll go down during the night."

"I hope so. That's kinda scary." Darlina walked to the kitchen and took the pan from the oven. "Why don't you keep it propped up? Maybe it will help. Think I should put a cold compress on it?"

"I'm scared to mess with the damn thing. The last thing I want is another open wound on a leg that can't heal."

A knot of worry formed in the pit of Darlina's stomach. How much more could Luke take at seventy-four?

She kept a close watch through the weekend, and by Sunday evening, the blister had grown to the size of a small cantaloupe.

"Baby, I really think I should take you to the ER in Abilene and get someone to look at this. I'm worried."

"You're probably right. Maybe they'll page the doc or he'll be on call. This thing is getting bigger by the minute."

Darlina packed a small bag just in case they put Luke in the hospital and loaded his scooter in the van.

When they reached the hospital, she parked in the Emergency Room parking lot and they hurried inside. After explanations and waiting, they finally put Luke in a small cubicle and paged Dr. Hudson, who happened to be the on-call doctor.

Two hours passed before he arrived. He took one look at the leg and sprang into action. "We need to drain this and bandage it. Fluid has seeped through your skin and formed this blister."

"Is it going to leave an open wound, Doc?"

"I will tell you this. When I drain the blister, it's highly likely the stretched skin won't adhere back to the leg. I can't say for sure, but there's a great chance of a large open wound. I'm also going to prescribe a diuretic to get off any more fluid you might be holding."

Darlina didn't dare breathe while the doctor drained the blister. Thoughts flew through her mind. Words like 'large open wound' rolled around like loose marbles clanking together.

They already knew circulation in the leg was bad. What would all of this mean?

She forced herself to take a breath and push the thoughts aside. No need in visualizing a situation that might not occur.

One glance read Luke's face. Even though he tried to keep a lighthearted attitude, she could clearly see the worry etched around his eyes.

They returned home that evening with a freshly bandaged leg and instructions to make an appointment with wound care the next day.

Once they were in bed, Darlina turned to Luke. "Honey, it's going to be all right. I'll get an appointment with Dr. Buman tomorrow. Maybe they can heal this up."

"I sure hope so. I don't know if I'm ready to lose another leg." He stared at a place on the wall over her head.

"All we can do is stay positive and get wound care started."

They both fell silent and the flickering lights from the TV bounced off the walls. That night, Darlina held Luke a little tighter. Neither of them slept much. Worry can do that to you.

Early the next morning, Darlina called the wound care center, and when the nurse told them to come immediately after hearing the situation, she called her workplace. She was relieved when Elora offered to help with her caseload.

Then she called Dr. Robertson's office and spoke to Becky, his nurse. Dr. Robertson would meet them in the hospital lobby at noon.

The situation called for immediate action and urgency.

***

After Dr. Buman's examination, he faced Luke. "Mr. Stone, we've been down this road before but since we have a much earlier start this time, I feel like we might be able to contain it. I do want to order a Doppler scan on the leg to see exactly what we're dealing with as far as blood flow. I'll prescribe antibiotics and I want to get you started with daily Hyperbaric treatments. We'll know within ten treatments whether it's going to help."

Darlina fought to stop the whirling thoughts in her brain. Daily trips to Abilene, more antibiotics, more struggle. She couldn't help questioning how much more Luke could take. And, even though she'd never admit it to anyone, how much more could she take?

Luke turned to Darlina. "Hell, baby, we'll figure out some way to get me back and forth every day without you having to take off work." He turned back to Dr. Buman. "I'll try anything, Doc."

Darlina reached for Luke's hand. "We'll do whatever we need to."

"I think we stand a half-decent chance if there's enough circulation," Dr. Buman reassured them.

With Luke in the hyperbaric chamber, Darlina met with Dr. Buman's nurse and scheduled a Doppler scan for the afternoon.

At least they weren't dragging their feet on this. Everyone knew the danger and risk involved.

She wouldn't allow herself to think about Luke facing another amputation. Surely, it would heal.

She had to believe that it would.

Miracles still happened and Luke deserved one. They couldn't take another surgery or another setback. She had to believe.

Nicole and Paul wedding

Chapter 26

F ollowing the ten Hyperbaric treatments, Luke had been hospitalized twice for I.V. antibiotics, yet the wound on his leg only worsened.

Once again, doctors prescribed antibiotic cream laced with a strong pain reliever and once again, Luke took medication to keep the constant agony at bay.

Andrew's third birthday was coming soon and Darlina wasn't sure Luke would be up to going to Dallas. There'd even been talk that Nicole and Paul might possibly fly from Denver, so of course that enticed them even more. But, Darlina didn't say anything. It would be up to Luke. She honestly didn't think he could make the trip. She could see him slipping more and more each day. Her heart ached inside her chest.

They sat in the living room, mid-February, Darlina perched in her favorite spot on the arm of Luke's chair, when Luke turned to her with a somber face. "Sweetheart, this may be the last chance I have to see our girls and it's important to me. I know it'll be a rough trip, but I want to go."

She fought tears. Seemed like she'd done that a lot over the past two months. "Then we'll go and I'll do everything in my power to make it as easy as possible."

He kissed her fingertips. "I know you will. I don't know for sure what we're facing with this leg, but I do know it could possibly be bad. I want to see the baby and the girls."

"I'll let Lily know."

Although Darlina worried that the trip might prove too much, if Luke wanted to try it, who was she to disagree? Happiness was fleeting enough with the best of circumstances and if she could help give him a little more, then that's what she'd do.

On the last Friday evening in February, Darlina loaded the van with the growing amount of medical supplies for Luke as well as an overnight bag and change of clothes. Worry gnawed at her. She'd called Lily when Luke was out of earshot and expressed her fear. Lily assured her mother she would do everything possible to make her dad comfortable.

They set out just as the sun was setting, with Darlina driving. Conversation was lean. Luke kept the CD player going and his left hand wrapped around Darlina's right.

They arrived in Dallas to find that Lily and Alexander had made a ramp for Luke to enter the house. Their thoughtfulness warmed Darlina's heart.

She and Luke were saddened when Lily reported that Nicole had phoned and wouldn't be there, but Andrew was thrilled to see his Gran and PaPa.

How he loved sitting on PaPa's lap and riding on the red scooter. He especially loved honking the horn and giggled every time.

On Saturday, a full-fledged turning three birthday celebration took place. How Darlina loved watching Andrew's eyes light up when he saw his cake. She and Luke clapped for him and encouraged him to open his presents.

Darlina kept a watchful eye on Luke relieved that so far, he'd managed okay, although he'd doubled up on the pain pills. It seemed to her that the fresh life in the child helped fill a void in Luke.

As the day turned into afternoon, Luke anxiously watched a weather report on TV. A snowstorm was moving in. He turned to Darlina. "Sugar, I know we planned to stay another night, but I'm afraid if we do, we won't be able to get back home. I think we need to head out."

Darlina nodded. "I hate to leave, but you're probably right." She headed to the bedroom, packed their things and with Lily and Alexander's help, loaded everything back into the van to head west.

Just as Luke was transferring from the wheelchair to the car seat, Lily gave her dad a hug and with tears in her eyes choked out. "I love you, Dad."

Luke cleared his throat. "I love you too, sweetheart. Take care of that baby for me and look out for your mother."

Lily nodded then turned and wrapped her arms around her mother. "Call me when you get home."

Darlina picked up Andrew and held him so that Luke could hug him, then she hugged the child and handed him to Lily.

Her voice quivered when she spoke. "I'll let you know when we are home."

Lily nodded hugging Andrew close.

Darlina swiped at tears as she backed out of the driveway. When she dared a glance at Luke, she didn't miss the stray tear that trickled down his cheek. She reached for his hand and in the lightly falling snow, drove the three hours back to Coleman.

***

On Monday, March 4th, Dr. Buman admitted Luke back into the hospital for another 10 day round of IV antibiotics and in-patient wound treatment.

Maybe this time they would start to see improvement.

Darlina packed a bag and drove Luke to the hospital. She made arrangements at work for the time off and was thankful that she still had vacation and sick days to draw from and even more thankful for Elora who assured her she would help. She didn't want to leave Luke's side. Whatever amount of precious time they had left, it wouldn't be wasted.

Each day, the wound care team came to his hospital room to take him to the Hyperbaric Chamber and change the dressing on his leg. As the pain increased, the doctor switched from pain pills to morphine. Luke battled with all his might and to Darlina, the unfairness of it all overwhelmed her.

She watched him grow weaker as time went on. Bedsores began to form on his backside and doctors ordered a special air bed for him, in order to slow their progress.

As always in hospitals, the weekends were the worst. Doctors were scarce, a new team of nurses arrived and the hustle and bustle of week days slowed to a low hum.

On Sunday, March 9th, Darlina knew something wasn't right. Luke shivered under the covers, even though the thermostat said it was seventy-five degrees in the room. She felt his forehead.

It was slightly warm, but not overly hot. However, she knew Luke well enough to know that he never registered a fever like a normal person. As the day turned to night, another nurse came on duty.

When she entered Luke's room making her rounds, Darlina expressed her concern. "He seems to be running a fever and hasn't been himself today," she whispered not wanting to disturb Luke.

The nurse nodded and took his temperature. "It's nothing to be alarmed about. It is just barely above normal. I'll bring another blanket."

Throughout the night, Darlina watched as Luke sank farther and farther into a state of disorientation. He muttered things that didn't make sense and shivered as if he stood on an iceberg. At times, he'd try to get out of bed.

Twice, Darlina brought the nurse in to check him and twice, she ignored the signs that Darlina knew too well.

Finally, as dawn broke, Darlina placed a call to Dr. Robertson's answering service. "Will you please have Dr. Robertson come to Luke Stone's room at the hospital as soon as possible?"

"I'll get the message to him," the voice on the other end assured.

She didn't know what else to do but stand watch and try to soothe Luke.

At seven that morning, the respiratory therapist arrived to give Luke a breathing treatment. He took one look at him and sprang into action.

"I'm afraid he's developed pneumonia, Mrs. Stone. I'm going to get the doctor on the phone right away."

Within minutes, a technician wheeled in an x-ray machine and took pictures of Luke's lungs. Less than an hour later, they brought in a Ventilator and placed a mask over Luke's face.

"This will force oxygen into his lungs," the man told Darlina.

At nine a.m., Dr. Robertson walked into the room. He took one look at Luke then turned to Darlina. "What happened?"

Darlina rubbed her hand across her forehead. "He's developed pneumonia. They said it was most likely caused by him being in bed so long and the morphine. They've taken him off morphine until he is better. I don't know how he will stand the pain," she whispered

Dr. Robertson laid his hand on Darlina's shoulder. "He's tough. This won't be easy though. I'm glad you called me. While I'm here, I'll take a listen to his heart."

"Thank you," she said weakly. Exhaustion overtook her and after Dr. Robertson left, she laid down on the narrow pull-out bed beside Luke's. She needed sleep.

Two hours later, the wound care team came in to change the dressing on Luke's leg. Darlina watched with tear-filled eyes as Luke groaned and writhed when they pulled the gauze away from the deteriorating flesh.

When tears squeezed out of the corner of his eyes, she couldn't bear it. "Isn't there anything you can give him for pain?"

"Not until he is breathing better. We're applying an extra layer of pain cream to the wound. Maybe that will help."

Once they reapplied the bandage, Luke settled down and seemed to sleep. Darlina lay back on the small bed and let her tears fall into the pillow.

Every sound woke her and after a while, she sat up and reached for a pencil and paper. She glanced over at Luke as she wrote. Silent sorrow dripped onto the paper.

Surrender
There is no shame in surrender when it is time
Like General Lee, you've known when to lay low
and when to climb
I've watched you suffer for so many years
Your life seemed destined to one of pain and of tears
Yet you fought on – the valiant soldier in fierce battle
You sang your song, rode tall in the saddle
You've now come down to the last battle call
You'll hang up your sword, tired and weary you'll fall
But know that you've left many good marks behind
While you learned how to love and how to be kind
Taught lessons to all who shared your many paths
That will be remembered long after you have passed
There is no shame in surrender when it is time

***

For the next forty-eight hours, it was touch and go. Once in a while Luke would open his eyes and silently plead with her through them.

All she could do, was hold his hand and stroke his head. She'd never felt so helpless in her entire life. And, she'd never been so exhausted.

After several days of the machine pushing air into Luke's lungs and antibiotics coursing through the IV, he began to breathe easier. On the fourth day, they removed the machine.

Once everyone had left the room, Darlina read the poem aloud. Her voice broke as she read. When she finished, Luke weakly reached for her hand.

Darlina squeaked. "Baby, I truly thought I'd lost you. You were so sick."

His voice was weak, "I thought you'd lost me too. I drifted in and out of a place that was very peaceful. But, when they would come and change the dressing on that leg with no pain-killers, I prayed to die."

"I agonized with you. I begged them to give you some-thing."

"When air hit the skin, it felt like a hot iron searing my leg."

Darlina leaned over the bed and placed a kiss on Luke's dry cracked lips. "You're going to get better." She reached for a container of Carmex.

He followed the trail of her finger on his parched lips. "Would you read the poem one more time?"

"Of course." She reached for the paper and slowly read the words again.

"General Lee was the greatest man that ever lived, but he did know when to pull back and when to surrender. I will too, but this wasn't it."

She let the paper fall from her hands and whispered, "Thank God."

Chapter 27

By April, the insurance company stopped paying for in-patient wound-care treatments and the doctor suggested they admit Luke to a nursing home in Abilene, explaining how that would make it convenient to continue the treatments.

Darlina stared at the doctor with a set mouth. "I will not put Luke in a nursing home. As long as I am alive, I will take care of him."

Luke narrowed his eyes. "Yeah, I'm not going into some damned nursing home. We can drive back and forth from Coleman."

The doctor shrugged his shoulders. "If you change your mind, I can make arrangements for you."

"We won't," Darlina said firmly.

When he left, Darlina turned to Luke. "Okay, baby, here's what I think we need to do. Because of the way the trailer is laid out, I think we should set up a hospital bed in the living room. As weak as you are and as much as it hurts to be on that leg, you can't hobble back and forth to the bedroom. I know the right people at work to go through to get what we need."

"Whatever makes it easier for you, baby. Damn, I hate the hardship all of this puts on you."

She placed her fingers across his lips. "Shh. Don't say that. I'm doing okay. Now that you're past the pneumonia, I have hope again."

"Yeah, I do too, until I look down and see the rotted flesh of my leg when they take the bandage off. But, I'm not ready to give up the fight yet."

"Neither am I. So, I'll get on the phone and see what I can do. We might also look at some home health care, someone to at least check in on you while I'm at work."

"A babysitter?" Luke said jokingly.

"Of sorts. I just don't want you there by yourself. We can make this work."

Luke grabbed her hand as she turned to leave. "I love you."

She went back to the bed. "I love you too. Don't ever forget it."

***

The living room of the trailer resembled a makeshift hospital room by the time Luke was discharged. Darlina had arranged for a hospital bed, rolling food tray, potty and a home health nurse to make Luke comfortable.

She saw how weak Luke had grown, when he could not pull himself up into the van. The male nurse assisting them had to position himself under Luke and push. Darlina watched with some apprehension. How would she be able to lift him? Well, she would figure it out because that is what she did.

She made arrangements to work half-days. Then she would take Luke to Abilene for treatments every afternoon. A home health nurse would check on him during the morning hours, change the dressing on his leg and take his vitals.

The only thing Darlina hadn't managed to resolve was where she would sleep. She'd thought she could sleep in a chair, but Luke wouldn't hear of it. She was afraid to go all the way back to the bedroom; afraid she wouldn't hear him if he called for her during in the night.

Luke's cousin brought a solution...a roll-away bed that she insisted Darlina use.

Through a home health program, Darlina hired a friend, Allie, to spend the morning hours with Luke. She promised to make sure he ate and to have him ready to go to Hyperbarics every day when Darlina came home.

As the days turned into weeks, Luke grew more frail. He could no longer lift himself from the wheelchair to the bed without assistance and Darlina wasn't strong enough to put him in the van. So, she relied on friends and family. Each day at noon, someone would be at the house to help her put Luke into the van. The outpouring of love touched Darlina's heart.

They did this for four weeks.

When Dr. Buman saw a worsening condition of the large bedsores on his backside and streaks starting up the leg, he hospitalized Luke again.

This time, with stronger IV antibiotics, there was only a small hope of slowing down the infection.

Darlina felt a sinking helpless feeling when they admitted Luke back into the hospital for the third time in as many months. She saw the deterioration every time they changed the bandage. She was losing Luke one piece at a time and her heart broke into a million pieces over and over again.

Luke's pain had gone from unbearable to excruciating. Each day seemed to bring a new level of pure agony.

The doctors came and went with no solutions.

They prescribed Morphine again and Luke was able to get short temporary reprieves from the misery. But, it never lasted long enough.

Time slowed down to a crawl. Life was measured in breaths and each breath came with a price.

Luke had been back in the hospital for a week, when the same doctor who'd done the amputation on the left leg strolled into the hospital room.

Darlina's heart froze like a block of granite inside her chest. She clutched the cup of coffee in her hand so hard the Styrofoam caved. She quickly tossed it into the nearby trash can.

"Mr. Stone, do you remember me?" He shook Luke's hand.

"Of course, Doc. No offense, but it's not a good memory."

The doctor chuckled. "Dr. Buman, Dr. Robertson and Dr. Hudson have consulted with me and feel that you are left with no choice but another amputation."

Luke stared past him with his jaw set. "And what if I don't agree?"

"The infection will spread up your leg and hit your organs, shutting them down."

"And I'll die." Luke's stare never faltered.

Darlina rose from the chair and came to stand beside the bed. With trembling fingers, she reached for Luke's hand.

"Yes. That's what will happen. It is inevitable."

"And if I have the leg taken off?"

"Then you stand a 50/50 chance of recovery. I recommend you choose the amputation."

"Doc, how would you like to be stuck living with no legs?"

"Mr. Stone, I have patients who have undergone this surgery and manage to go on living full lives."

Bitterness crept into Luke's reply. "Well, they ain't me." He looked at Darlina. "I won't put more burdens on Darlina than I already have."

The doctor turned to Darlina. "I won't sugarcoat it. If he survives another surgery, there will be a long recovery period."

She wondered where all of the ever-present tears had suddenly gone. She felt calm and confident. "Whatever Luke wants, I will stand beside him."

"Talk it over and make a decision. The only other option I can suggest is maybe hospice."

"Aren't they the people who help you die?" Luke asked.

The doctor's voice was quiet. "Yes."

"We'll talk about it all."

"Fine. I'll be back tomorrow."

Once he left, Darlina leaned over the bed and laid her head on Luke's chest. "Oh Luke. What are we going to do?"

He stroked her hair. "Sugar, you know I'd do anything to stay here with you, but I can't stand to be more of an invalid than I already am. I don't want to live without any legs."

She raised her head and looked into his watery blue eyes. "You know I'll always do my best to take care of you."

"I know, but look at what I've already put you through."

"You've put yourself through far worse. What I've done, I'd do all over again a million times. There is nothing stronger than our love…Nothing."

"There are so many things I've left half-done. If only I could have a few more years." The words ended with a sigh. "Would you climb up here beside me?"

"Of course." She slipped her shoes off and gingerly raised herself up on the bed and snuggled next to him. She cradled his head against her breast.

Sobs shook Luke's shoulders. "I'll never be totally gone. You know that don't you? I'll always be with you."

Darlina sobbed with him. "I know."

Words became inadequate.

When the nurse came in an hour later, they didn't move. Wrapped in each other's arms with streaks of tears on both of their faces, they clung to their love and the last few grains of sand in the hourglass.

"I'll come back in a little while." She tiptoed out the door.

Finally Darlina spoke with a quivering voice. "Baby, you're leaving behind a legacy of so many songs, writings and poems for me to do something with. I promise that I will keep trying to promote them however I can for as long as I am alive."

Luke sighed. "I hope that somewhere in all of it, there is one treasure. You deserve good things in life. It would make me very happy to know that I left something worthwhile behind."

When the nurse returned, Darlina got off the bed and reached for tissues. She wiped her face and blew her nose and handed one to Luke.

After she'd left, Luke continued. "Let's talk to the hospice people tomorrow. I don't know if it's what we need, but it can't hurt to talk. I damned sure don't like the other option."

"I'll tell someone at the nurse's station."

When she stepped out of the room to request a hospice meeting, she saw Elora getting off the elevator.

She couldn't hold back the tears. "Elora, Luke has asked me to set up a meeting with hospice. The doctor left a little while ago and said we either have to do another amputation or possibly get set up with hospice."

Elora put her arms around Darlina. "I'm so sorry. You know, I had a feeling things weren't going good. I just had to come and see you and Luke."

"Will you go in with him while I talk to the nurse?"

"Of course."

Darlina hugged her friend and walked down the hallway to the nurse's station.

When she came back into the room, Luke was laughing and telling jokes with Elora. She was the perfect person to come into the grave situation.

As visiting hours drew to a close, Elora promised to come back in the morning. Her visit had been a good distraction for Luke.

While Darlina had been out of the room, she'd also taken time to make calls to both of the girls to let them know what was going on. Nicole said she would catch the next plane out and Lily promised to be up the next day. Then she called Martin. He also promised to catch a flight within the next couple of days.

She felt like she was gathering the troops. Maybe she was.

Off and on, throughout the night, Luke and Darlina talked. Twice, Darlina got back in bed with him. They both needed the comfort and closeness.

The next morning three women came into Luke's room and introduced themselves. "We're from hospice. We understand you and your wife want to talk to us."

Luke pushed himself up in the bed. "I suppose we do. The surgeon wants to take this other leg off and I'm just not willing to go through that. I'm seventy-four years old with a bad heart and I don't want to live with no legs. He said my other option was hospice. So, I guess that's you."

Darlina introduced herself and gathered chairs for everyone. Again, she was very thankful that Elora had come back to be with them that morning. Her steady calmness was what they needed.

One of the women explained what hospice was and the services they could provide.

After the lengthy explanation, Luke turned to the woman. "Can your doctors get me out of this pain?"

"Yes sir."

"You're telling me that your doctors can give me enough medicine that I don't hurt anymore?"

"Yes sir."

He turned to Darlina. "Sign me up."

Darlina gasped. Reality set in. Luke was choosing to die. "Are you sure, Luke?"

"I've never been more sure about anything in my life."

"Okay." She turned to the woman. "What do I do?"

"Come with me and we'll get all of the paperwork in order."

A sob escaped Darlina's throat. She turned to Elora. "Can you stay with Luke until I get back?"

"Of course. That's why I'm here."

Darlina followed the woman out of the room and down the hallway to a small office. One by one, Darlina blindly signed papers that were placed in front of her. She had no idea what they said. All she knew was that this was what Luke wanted. He was choosing to die and she was helping him.

She could no more have stopped the tears from streaming down her face than she could have willed her heart to stop beating.

When she returned to Luke's room, eyes red and swollen, she was greeted with laughter. Yes, Elora was the perfect person to buffer this moment. Luke needed someone who could laugh with him. At this point in time, it wasn't her. All she could do was cry.

He looked up when she walked in. "All done?"

"All done. The woman said their doctor would be in see you before the end of the day. She also said they'll put you in a coma so anything else you need to tell me, now is the time."

Elora stood. "I have to get back to work." She walked to Luke's bed and leaned over. "See you on the other side, my friend."

Darlina followed her into the hallway. "Thank you so much for being here. I'll let you know when it's over."

"Keep your chin up. This is what he wants and he's at peace with it."

"I know," Darlina whispered. She watched until her friend reached the elevator and turned on wooden legs back to Luke's room.

"I need to see Mark and Jerry. Can you call them?" Luke asked.

"Of course." She reached for the phone and dialed. When she hung up, she said, "Jerry said he'll be here in twenty minutes. Also, both of the girls and Martin are on their way."

"That's good. You're going to need them." Luke reached out his hand to her. "Baby, none of this is easy, but I'm tired. Tired of hurting, tired of being in this damned bed with bedsores that hurt almost as bad as the leg, and tired of watching you walk around exhausted. So, I'm gonna fix that."

She came to him. "I wish there was some other way."

"There is, but all it would do is prolong the misery for both of us. I'm ready to get it over with. I'm not afraid."

Within two hours, Lily arrived. Darlina left the room so she could be alone with the man who'd raised her as his own. She knew they had things to say. Throughout the day, everyone Luke needed to see came. Darlina watched it all unfold like a movie scene. Nothing seemed real.

***

On Friday, April 24th, an ambulance transported Luke from Abilene to their home in Coleman.

He was groggy, but still coherent when they arrived. Darlina followed in the van. She forced herself to stop thoughts and simply drive. There was nothing else to consider except keeping Luke comfortable.

Once they arrived, she assisted the hospice nurse in getting Luke settled. Even though his eyes were open, Darlina could see him disconnecting from his surroundings.

After specific instructions on how to administer the medication, the nurse left. Friends began to stop by, each needing to have one last word with the man who meant so much to them.

Darlina appreciated them all and felt something almost like terror when the last one left and she was alone, completely responsible for Luke's care.

In a lucid moment, Luke asked Darlina to wipe down his treasured guitar and put it in its case for safekeeping. Again, she moved as if in a dreamlike trance; not feeling, only moving.

She placed the morphine pills under his tongue as the nurse instructed and as evening fell, she set an alarm to give him more medicine every four hours.

The night turned into a struggle with Luke being half in and half out of consciousness. Several times, he tried to get out of bed. Darlina felt thankful he was weak enough that she could constrain him. By early morning, she made a call to hospice. She needed help. He thrashed around and moaned, obviously not at ease.

Within an hour, a nurse arrived. She administered a shot and he calmed.

After different medication instructions, the nurse left. The time interval had been increased to every two hours. The nurse assured her this would keep Luke comfortable.

Darlina spent hours sitting beside him, sometimes dozing with her head on the side of his bed.

Finally, Nicole arrived and shortly afterward, Martin made it in. With the young baby, and now pregnant with her second child, Lily made the decision not to return. She had said her farewells to her father when they visited at the hospital. Darlina assured her it was the right thing to do. Andrew would not understand what was wrong with PaPa and how could you explain it to a three year old?

Throughout the week, family and friends stopped in to sit with Luke, talk to him and share any last thought they had despite the fact that he never opened his eyes again.

On the third day, Luke began to gurgle when he gasped for a breath. The nurses told her this was called the death rattle.

When she heard the term, she instantly conjured up a vision of the ancient Medicine Men and Shamans dancing around a sacred fire shaking rattles. She hoped they were with Luke now, comforting and assisting him on this journey.

And yet the days dragged on. Darlina would occasionally go to their bedroom and rest for a couple of hours when someone else sat with Luke. He was not to be left alone for even a minute.

Each of his children came as the week progressed, including his sons, Nathan and Joseph. Nicole and Martin stayed and Lily called several times daily.

In the late night hours of April 30th, Darlina's friend Sally arrived. She'd driven from East Texas and gotten in around midnight.

"You look exhausted, Darlina. Get some sleep and I'll sit with Luke. I need to talk to him anyway."

Darlina nodded and lay down on the roll-away bed. She drifted off to sleep, only to awaken a couple of hours later.

She stretched her sore and stiff muscles and joined Sally at Luke's bedside. "I don't know what he's waiting on. Everyone has been here to say their farewells, but he's waiting for something or someone."

Sally agreed. "Each breath is a struggle. I think he knows I'm here, though."

"They told us that he would be aware of everyone around him, but that he just can't respond." She stroked Luke's forehead. "I'm going to step outside and get a breath of fresh air."

"Go ahead. I'll be here."

Darlina opened the side door of the trailer that led to the carport and stepped outside.

That space of time between night and day, held a still coolness of early spring. The scent of blooming honeysuckle and Luke's beloved roses filled the air. She put her hands behind her head and stretched her back.

The boys were asleep next door in the empty building that had been The Saturday Store and Nicole was asleep in her room.

What was Luke waiting for? Everyone had gathered to help him.

She remembered what Luke had told her many times. *'When I pass from this life you'll hear two sounds. You'll hear a train whistle blowing and you'll hear an owl hooting.'*

She'd thought of that frequently over the past few days. The train whistle was a regular occurrence since the tracks were no more than a mile away. And she'd heard the whistles blow often. But, the owls hadn't come.

She took a deep breath and gazed up at the clear Texas sky and twinkling stars.

Another train passed by. The whistle moaned its lonesome sound.

Then she heard it. Somewhere nearby, an owl hooted. The hair stood up on the back of her neck.

Without thinking, she turned and hurried back through the door, not bothering to close it. She walked straight to Luke's bed, leaned in close to his ear and whispered, "The owls are here, honey. It's time."

In less than five minutes, Luke took in a long gasp and let out a sigh, then nothing else.

Darlina saw a cloud-like mist float across the room and exit through the side door.

She looked at Sally with complete calm. "It's over."

Sally simply nodded.

"We'll need to call someone."

Again Sally nodded.

Darlina turned toward the shelf in the den that held the Sweetgrass. Moving, as if in a trance, she reached for the ceramic container and pulled out the rope.

After lighting it, she waved it over Luke's still body. His face lost all signs of struggle and age.

There were no tears, only total calm.

She felt feathers brush against her skin and encircle her. Angel wings.

Luke was finally free. No more pain, no more struggle, nothing more to prove. His last song had been sung.

She reached for the phone to call hospice, then went to wake up Luke's sons while Sally awoke Nicole.

Darlina still felt totally encompassed in a peaceful embrace. As she walked next door to wake up the boys, she wondered why she'd been compelled to leave the side door open after hearing the owls.

Without question, Luke's spirit left through that open door...Left to join his owl brothers, his family and his creator.

In less than an hour, the hospice nurses arrived and by early morning, the funeral home came to claim the body for cremation.

Darlina sat quietly with Sally and the children in the den when they heard the zipper close on the body bag.

As they wheeled Luke out on the narrow stretcher, they all stood as if paying tribute to a fallen soldier.

Then came the tears. They came in selfish shattering waves from somewhere deeper than the mind or body. They came from the soul.

Luke Stone had fought his last fight.

THE END

Death leaves a heartache no one can heal
Love leaves a memory no one can steal
Goodbye is not forever
Goodbye is not the end
It simply means that I'll miss you
Until we meet again
And we will meet again
          ~From a headstone in Ireland~

Luke Stone waving goodbye

Epilogue

I remained in Coleman for six months following Luke's passing. The world we'd worked so hard to build was empty and void without him.

So, I packed up our entire lifetime into boxes and stored the memories away in my heart. I transferred my job and moved close to Lily. I listed the Coleman property on the market and in 2012, new owners moved in.

As was so often said, I thought someone would come along who would write mine and Luke's story. I awoke one morning to the stark realization that I was the only one who really knew what happened. Therefore I had to be the author. I chose to tell the story through fictitious characters simply because that was the only way for me to separate myself enough to be able to tell it the way it needed to be told.

The result is a series of four books which span a time period from 1971 to 2009, *Flowers and Stone*, *The Convict and the Rose*, *Home at Last* and *'Til Death Do Us Part*. It is my deepest hope that somehow through relating these stories, another person will be inspired to reach a little higher, dream a little bigger and love a little deeper.

I currently reside in North Texas, have five grandchildren, and live within two miles of both Lily and Nicole.

Writing these books has been an incredible journey. I have laughed, cried, struggled and triumphed through the process. I'd like to thank everyone who encouraged and supported me on this venture and those who gave me permission to use their real names in the stories.

As I close this chapter of my life, I look forward to whatever adventures lie ahead.

If you have enjoyed reading *'Til Death Do Us Part*, I humbly ask that you take a moment to post an honest review on the on-line sale site of your choice, (Amazon, Barnes & Noble) or on Goodreads. Reviews are the best way for readers to discover new books.

From the bottom of my heart, thank you for taking this odyssey with me. Stay in touch!

Jan Sikes (aka Darlina Stone)

~RECIPES~

Rick's heart disease was long and extensive starting in February 1989, with an open heart surgery in which he had five bypasses. Over the years, he had several stents and other various medical procedures including two Fem-Popliteal Bypass Grafts on the left leg, each done one year apart. He eventually lost that leg to amputation.

He had Atherosclerosis (which the old-timers used to call hardening of the arteries). Our cardiologist sent him to Lubbock in 1996 to be evaluated for a possible heart transplant. That doctor told him he was not a candidate for a heart transplant since his disease was in all of the arteries and veins throughout the body. He stressed that diet was the only possible hope for living 'maybe' another 6 months. That was when I got inspired to do the research and work of putting a diet together, making it as low-fat as possible, but maintaining good nutrition and taste.

I believe the fact that he lived thirteen more years, after being told he only had another six months, was directly due to the diet. In February 2009, before passing away in May 2009, it had been twenty years since the first heart by-pass surgery. The cardiologist said the normal life of a bypass is 10 to 12 years. So, again, I believe the low fat diet helped us surpass those odds greatly.

I want to share a few of my recipes with you to end this series and hope you take away some tid-bit from this segment into your own life.

The first thing I had to cut from Rick's diet was anything fried. I experimented with several different methods before finding the one that worked every time without fail.

One large bag of fat-free pretzels ground into a fine meal, (much like the consistency of corn meal) using an ordinary blender, worked wonders as a coating. If you have a food processor this will be even easier to get the consistency you want.

For meats such as chicken, venison or fish, beat to a foamy consistency, three to four egg whites (you can now purchase egg whites in cartons). Dip small pieces into the egg whites then roll them in the pretzel meal. Spray with PAM on both sides and bake at 425 degrees for 20 minutes, turning each piece once after ten minutes. The result will be crispy oven-fried food. If you have a Convection oven, you will not need to turn the pieces as they will cook on both sides at the same time.

For dryer things such as shrimp, eggplant, onion slices, sliced yellow or zucchini squash, I found that fat-free plain yogurt with a small amount of warm water added to achieve the consistence of buttermilk worked beautifully. Dip the slices into the yogurt mixture then roll in pretzel meal, spray both sides with PAM and bake at 425 degrees for approximately 15 minutes.

Another thing Rick loved, was large Portabella Mushrooms oven-fried. For those, I used the egg white dip to coat the slices, and rolled them in Pretzel meal. He said they were a meat replacement for him as far as texture and taste.

Jan's Oatmeal Pancakes

1/4 C Egg Beaters (or can substitute with one egg)

1 Pkg any flavor of Weight Control Quaker Instant Oatmeal

1/2 C Whole Wheat Flour

1/2 C Applesauce

1 tsp Baking Powder

1/4 C Chopped Walnuts

1/4 C Dried Blueberries or Raisins

Mix together, spray griddle with PAM and cook until done.

Makes Two servings.

Nutritional Value per serving:

Calories 250

Fat 7 Grams

Saturated Fat 0

TransFat 0

Polyunsat 3

Cholesterol 0

Carbs 29

Fiber 6

Sugar 11

Protein 10 Grams

Jan's Faux Coconut Pie

2 ½ Cups Spaghetti Squash
2 Eggs slightly beaten (equivalent amount of Egg Beaters)
½ Cup Sugar
½ Cup White Karo Syrup
2 ½ Tsp. Coconut Flavoring
½ Cup Chopped Pecans or Walnuts
Pinch of Salt

Open Spaghetti Squash and remove seeds. Put in Microwave safe dish with ¼ cup of water in bottom. Cover and cook each half of the squash approximately 10 minutes or until soft. Remove the squash from the shell and let cool.

Once cool, add all other ingredients, place into unbaked pie shell and bake at 350° for approximately 1 hour until set.

This replaces the high cholesterol and fat Coconut and yet maintains the texture and flavor of coconut pie!

Lentils and Rice

1 Cup Lentils
½ Cup Brown Rice
½ Onion diced
½ Green Bell Pepper diced
1 large carrot diced
1 tsp Garlic Powder
½ tsp Ground Cumin
Salt and pepper to taste

Rinse the lentils and place into 6 cups of boiling water. Add rice, onion, bell pepper and carrot. Cover and cook for one hour on low heat.
Makes Four servings

Nutrition:
Calories   312
Protein   17 Grams
Fat   0
Cholesterol 0

Serve with ½ C non-fat Cottage Cheese to add 14 Gr Protein, 0 Fat and 10 Mg. Cholesterol

GREEN PEA SALAD

1 Can Green Peas
1 boiled egg
¼ Cup diced onion
1 TBS Non-Fat Miracle Whip
Mix and chill
Nutrition:
Calories 70
Protein   13
Fat   0
Cholesterol .9 mg

SPICY UNFRIED FRIED POTATOES

Peel and slice potatoes just as you would if you were going to make real French Fries. If you're using red potatoes, scrub and slice, leaving the peel on.

Beat two egg whites until foamy.

Place the sliced potatoes in the egg whites and sprinkle Chili Powder, salt and pepper and mix well, being careful to get the egg white mixture on each potato slice.

Spray a cookie sheet with PAM and place the potatoes on it. Make sure each slice is lying flat. Spray the top of the potatoes with PAM and bake at 400 degrees for 45 min.

Necessity is of the mother of invention and because Rick loved fried potatoes so much, I came up with this substitute

COTTAGE CHEESE SPINACH CASSEROLE

2 C No-Fat Cottage Cheese
3 TBS Flour
4 Oz. No-Fat Ricotta Cheese
10 Oz. fresh Spinach
1 tsp. Onion Powder

Mix together and bake for 60 min. uncovered at 350 degrees.
Makes Four servings.
Calories   197
Protein   26 Gr.
Fat   0
Cholesterol 0

Banana Split Muffins

2 C Flour
¾ C Sugar
1 tsp. salt
1 tsp baking soda
1 egg
1 C Applesauce
3 Ripe Bananas mashed
1 C Chocolate Chips
1 C Dried Cherries

Pre-heat oven to 375 degrees.

In a medium bowl, combine flour, sugar, salt and baking soda. In another bowl, mix together the egg and applesauce. Add this mixture to the dry ingredients. Stir in bananas, chocolate chips and dried cherries.

Spoon batter into greased muffin pan until each muffin cup is almost full.

Bake 20 minutes or until lightly browned. Makes 12 muffins.

Coming Soon!

From the heart and soul of Rick and Jan Sikes,
thought provoking poetry along with his unique
style of pen-and-ink art

www.jansikes.com

A passionate love story set in the rowdy raucous honky-tonks of Texas in 1970. Luke Stone, veteran Texas musician has lost all reason to believe in himself or his music until he meets Darlina Flowers…

"This is a journey through words and music of two people facing struggles of epic proportion from shackles and chains to drugs and gurus with undying LOVE as their North Star."

www.jansikes.com

With empty pockets and a heart full of dreams Luke Stone leaves behind the nightmare of fifteen long years in Leavenworth prison.

A heartwarming journey of love, faith, hope and perseverance.

www.jansikes.com

About the Author

Multi-Award winning author, Jan Sikes, began her writing journey around the age of eight.

Primarily, the stories she writes are <u>true stories</u> about the journey of two people moving through adversity in order to grow and learn to become better humans. She believes with all her heart, there is something worth sharing in these stories. Bits and pieces of wisdom, hard-learned lessons and above and beyond all, love…True love that you read about in fiction stories…and yet this is truth. The old saying that *truth is stranger than fiction* fits the stories that she shares.

Passionate about her writing projects, Jan is driven to tell a deeply personal story with the hope that it might touch someone's heart or life in a positive way.

She also releases a music CD of original songs along with each book that fits the time period of the story. Why? Because the stories revolve and evolve around a deep-rooted passion for music.

Jan resides in North Texas, has five grandchildren and in her spare time, loves to volunteer at Texas music festivals. She serves on the Board of Directors for the Texas Musicians Museum, The North Texas Book Festival and the Texas Author's Institute of History.

www.ingramcontent.com/pod-product-compliance
Lightning Source LLC
Chambersburg PA
CBHW071104250626
47159CB00002B/589